Her Vicious Beasts

The Beginning

A Note on the Content

I care about the mental health of my readers.
This book contains some themes you might want to know about before you read.
They are listed at www.ektaabali.com/themes

E.P. Bali's House of Romantasy

Her Vicious Beasts: The Beginning is a work of fiction. Names, characters, places, incidents and locations are the product of the author's imagination or are used fictitiously. Any resemblance to actual events, locations or persons, living or dead is entirely coincidental.

This first edition published in 2023 by
Blue Moon Rising Publishing
www.ektaabali.com

ISBN ebook: 978-0-6456909-1-0
Paperback: 978-0-6456909-0-3
Hardback: 978-0-6457846-0-2

Cover Design by David Gardias
Book Formatting by E.P. Bali with Vellum

Her Vicious Beasts

The Beginning

E.P. Bali

Chapter 1

Aurelia

My vibrator is broken.

Pressing the on/off button aggressively over and over again does nothing. Neither does changing the batteries. I swear under my breath, tossing the cheap pink silicon towards the end of my bed where it bounces off my faded purple coverlet and onto the floor with a *thunk*, almost knocking over my huge stack of thrift store romance novels.

That tiny saviour of a device had been the cheapest I could find on my limited budget, and I can't afford to get a replacement. A heavy blow, to be sure.

Morning beams of sunlight stream through my tattered curtains and I fling an arm over my eyes for a single moment of mourning before I have to get up for the day.

An orgasm—fuelled by Draco and Hermione fan fiction—is the best way to recharge my powers, and the one highlight of my miserable days. I'll now have to settle for being a little lethargic and irritable until I can get back home tonight for a proper self-care session. My anima prowls under my skin, annoyed and demanding release, but the poor beast inside of me will just have to make do. She's been particularly jumpy lately, but I'm sure it's all to do with me leaving town soon.

Reaching for the phone on my bedside table, I open up my *Animalia Today* news app and check the latest:

A rabid wolf serial killer has finally been caught, many thanks to the Lioness Mums United Retrieval Team. His head is on display at the front of their headquarters for all to see.

Relations between the human population and Animalia are "better than ever" according to the Council's latest reports.

There's a missing dragon, heir to the Drakos line,

who appears to have gotten caught up in some underground crime ring.

The Deputy Headmaster of Animus Academy is being praised for his feral youth rehab program.

Political nonsense, *yada yada*. Council of Beasts ass kissing, *yada yada*.

Nothing new.

I only have two weeks of summer holidays left before I leave for college. An actual *human* college. For the first time in seven years, I'm actually excited about something. After I finished high school, I did an online course on advancing my healing skills where I did super well, so that got me a scholarship at an interstate college. My bags are already packed. I'm making a life for myself, *by* myself and I couldn't be prouder.

When I turned twenty earlier this year, I was officially an animalia adult meaning that freedom from my father is on the horizon. After moving states, I'll join the local branch of the Court of Wings and get to live my life away from him forever.

I only have to survive fourteen more days in my aunt's shop.

When I turned thirteen, my dad made an agreement—well, let's be real—had *ordered* my aunt that I was to work in her store every day after my schoolwork was done. Now that I no longer needed a guardian, I'm to work there until I leave for college. In exchange, I get a tiny allowance to cover food and am allowed to stay in this one-bedroom rustic affair, one huff and puff away from falling apart. The paint is peeling in every one of the three rooms and the living room ceiling leaks during even the lightest of rain, but it is mine to do with as I please.

Which is just as well because I'm not allowed to leave it for anything other than work.

It's a way for my father to keep me in my place. To show me where I belonged after I hit puberty and it was revealed that I'd taken my mother's genes and my anima was *not* a serpent like everyone had hoped. Father moved me out of home, I got kicked out of the Serpent Court, removed as serpent heir and put here, out of sight but still under his thumb.

I'm forbidden from speaking about my mother and the genes I inherited from her. In fact, I'm forbidden to speak to any animalia at all unless it involves one of the occasional jobs I do for my father.

But nothing can stop me now, and I grin at the thought of finally making some friends at college as I haul myself out of bed and into the bathroom. I just manage to shower and get my work clothes on before a tingle of warning shoots through me.

Someone is walking through the shield I've set at the perimeter of the house. I stand to attention, heart pounding, simply listening to the dreaded panging of my heart.

There is only one person in the entire world who could get past one of my house shields and simply walk onto this property.

Just one.

Chapter 2

Aurelia

Panicking, I dart from my bathroom into my tiny living room just in time to see the front door slam open and two of my father's lackeys skulk in. I stiffen, frozen to the spot as the two women, wiry and hunched, dressed in black overcoats and black jeans, check my house for threats, looking anywhere but me. They both wear black lipstick and heavy black eyeliner—the snakes of my father's court prefer a grunge style of fashion. In general, animalia always like to dress to the style of their order, so there are always telltale signs of what beast they are:

Lions always wear their hair long, often braided; males and females both.

Eagles and other birds choose spiky hair styles, mohawks and so on.

Wolves love denim on a religious level, and their men always wear short beards.

Part of this is so other animalia can discern who they're dealing with quickly. We can usually tell via scent, but human perfumes and other conflicting smells in public make that difficult.

With their tongues darting out, tasting the air in the habit of half feral reptiles, my dad's servants come to stand on either side of my front door.

I stand facing them in a sort of lame disbelief as two tall males come in next—security guards by the guns they openly carry at their waists. They give me a droll look before bracketing the women to stand against the wall, their arms crossed, eyes staring over my head.

My heart threatens to leap right out of my ribcage.

This is *very* bad.

He's come himself with his full contingent—as if I'm some foreign court member and this is a formal meeting. The warning bells are loud in my head. Either he has one last big job for me, or something much worse.

I haven't always feared him. He had been a good

father when his hopes for me were grand. But the same day my anima was revealed, he'd gone from doting father to cruel taskmaster in the space of minutes.

With his presence announced, my father comes in next, striding through the door in military-grade black boots. He is a wraith of a man, far too tall and far too lean, his cheeks hollowed out, deep bags under his eyes—as if the King Cobra bore some great worldly burden on his shoulders. But I know better. That was the weight of black magic, and he used it like an addict. We look a little similar, I suppose; I get my olive skin and dark hair from his side of the family and I'm thin from my diet of two-minute noodles and the rare poptart.

I haven't seen him for an entire year—his assistants text me his orders—but he doesn't look any different from the last time.

Those black eyes fix upon me like a predator's hunting gaze and I want to sink inside the ground and never be seen again. I can't help but notice he's standing just inside the doorstep, as if he's too disgusted to come in any further. As if it's beneath him to enter properly. I only have two weeks left until I'm out of his life. He couldn't have just left me alone?

"Aurelia." His voice slithers up my spine and I suppress a cringe.

"Father." I nod, keeping both my voice and face blank.

Both female scouts hiss with displeasure at my lack of use of his honorific, 'Your Highness'. If I were any other person, that would warrant a death blow, or in Serpent Court style, a call for slow execution via poison. He doesn't like it when I call him *'father'* or *'dad'*, because I could be no daughter of his. But in a world where complete submission is expected of me, calling him 'father' is the single act of defiance I allow myself.

The only sign of his displeasure is a twitch at the side of his mouth as he raises his hand to placate his lackey scumbags; the picture of a fair and benevolent ruler.

"Are you well?" he asks flatly, his eyes clinically darting around my body to check for signs of disability or disease. His dark presence falls upon me like a heavy blanket, and I suppress the urge to shift uncomfortably. I want him gone, out of my space and out of my life. I'm a legal adult now and not a part of his court—that surely means I have some autonomy. *Some* leg to stand on now.

"I am well," I confirm, and in a sudden burst of

uncharacteristic bravery I say, "What do you need, father? I need to get to work."

He takes a single step forward, and that movement has my heart skipping multiple beats. I can't help the fear rising in me and I am so ashamed of myself when I take a woeful step back in response.

His black eyes gleam at how much I'm acting like prey. "You will not be going to the shop today, Aurelia," he says.

I know he can feel my fear, taste it in the air, hear it in my heartbeat. But I can't control that right now. Not as they crowd my tiny house, not as my entire world narrows onto one realisation.

I *am* twenty now.

I am a woman in my father's eyes.

Perhaps going away to college was a fool's dream. The dream of a stupid, hopeful girl.

Is this it?

Is this my day of reckoning where my father reveals our secret for his own gain? Where he sells me like chattel to the highest bidder? The Old Laws permit it and there are many who still hold on to them.

"And why is that?" I hate the tremble in my voice.

"I have a colleague in need of your healing abilities."

Cool relief washes through me like a king tide and I know I visibly sag under the weight being released from the thought that I was being sold into marriage or a breeding pen. I let out a shaky breath, almost laughing out loud. He needs to let me go to college. I can't be doing his *tasks* anymore.

"You have access to better healers than—"

"You know that's not true." His voice interrupts me with a flash of his fangs. I shudder.

For a secondary power, I'm rather good at healing. While it's rare for a shifter to have a second power, I—like my mother—am a rare creature.

My father has kept me hidden so no one finds out exactly *how* rare I am. But all the same, it's taken years to become a good healer. To learn all the ins and outs of a shifter's body. Whenever my father wants me to help, it means the case is something unusual and dangerous no one else will touch. Something that will, no doubt, put me at risk.

"I'm twenty now," I blurt. "I'm not a part of your court. You can't order me anymore—"

His eyes flash in anger and he flings out his arm in a strike. The shadow of his huge serpent animus flies out of his palm head first. It hurtles through the air straight for me, its jaws dislocate, snap out, and find their place clamped around my neck. I choke on a scream, staggering backwards as sharp teeth pierce the delicate sides of my throat. My back thumps against the kitchen wall and I blink rapidly, trying to stay still as my father advances on me. His lackeys grin behind him.

This is why he is king of his court. It's easy for animalia to shift into our animal forms. To shift part of our body one at a time was rare. To remove the spirit of it and use it to attack someone else? Unheard of. It's unnatural. But *unnatural* is something serpents respect.

When my father speaks again, his voice is dangerously calm. "You will be given the name and address of the place I need you to go today. And you *will* go. Is that clear? I have already spoken to my sister."

I grind my teeth as the shadow-serpent squeezes its jaws around my neck, choking my blood supply. Stars erupt in my vision, making my father's face twinkle with faint lights. He looms over me, grim-faced; no love, no light in those black eyes. My heart splits in two all over again, and I understand just how naïve I've been.

His voice drops even lower. "I *said*, Aurelia, is that clear?"

I let out a sorry grunt. My age means nothing to him. It's no more than a legality. He will always own me. "Yes, father."

He turns on his heel and the serpent is ripped from my throat, disappearing back into my father's hand, leaving me reeling. I gasp, my knees buckling, and I collapse onto my kitchen tiles.

They leave in a procession and I watch them, a hand over my burning neck. The last—a female viper—turns and gives me a black-lipped smirk before she slams my front door shut, making my windows quiver in their frame, just like me.

I can't help the hot tears that slide from my eyes as I feel them all depart through my shield outside.

Fuck. Fuck. Fuck. I bring my hand away from my neck, and it's smeared with red. I stand on shaking legs and hobble to my mirrored kitchen splash-back, leaning down to check the damage. All seven of the personal shields I permanently keep around me are down—that's the effect my father has on me.

But it means I can see myself properly, and I'm forced to see my latent mating mark on the right side of my neck. It's a mark that only animalia from your mating group can see, marking you as soul-bound in all lifetimes. Animalia spend their entire lives looking for others with the same mark. Mine is a skull with five streams of light bursting from it.

And the five reasons I'm forced to live the hidden life that I do.

Oozing crimson dots line both sides of my neck. As angry tears burn the backs of my eyes, I heal them just enough to stop the bleeding.

I want those wounds to remain painful.

Because every time I feel that burn, I want to remember the type of man my father is. That one day, I *will* be free of him. Somehow. Some way.

My phone pings and I fish it out of my pocket to see that his assistant has texted me the address he wants me to go to. I sigh in resignation. Wherever this leads, it's not going to be good.

I fling all seven of my shields back up and watch my mating mark disappear along with my scent. Being hidden is how I will survive this life. What my father has left of it, anyway.

Chapter 3

Aurelia

I've been working odd jobs for my father since I was a child, even before my anima was revealed. Back then, he tread carefully, using these *jobs*—as he'd called them—to train my shielding and healing abilities to make me a powerful addition to his court; someone he can use to strengthen his hold over other beasts.

But once I'd been exiled from said court, the jobs became a little riskier, a little more dangerous. My father, being the King of Serpents, deals with the dangerous and wealthy. So they'd gone from simple healing tasks to life-threatening injuries after big fights, even *during* inter-court fights or underground fighting rings between valuable beasts. I'd often have to make myself invisible using my special eighth shield, so no one knew I was there. It made my father a sort of enigma, that he could promise powerful healing but no one knew by what means. I think they all assumed he used some type of black magic from a distance.

I'm sure he got paid well for my services.

Since my father forbade me from getting a proper job, I had thought about taking up human sex work for money to generate an income. A side-hustle. Stripping was too public, but I could possibly make money quickly selling my body. Any money I made I would have to hide from him, so cash payments were my best option, and in addition, I'd get a power boost. I never got the courage to follow through with that idea, though it would have really helped me recharge some days, I'm sure.

They'd messaged me the location of one 'Mr. G. Halfeather,' and the address of a property a little way from town—an area I'm not familiar with. It can't be an illegal cage fight or a battle for territory. The former are in locations well known to me and the latter are always in Council-approved fields or warehouses. In addition, the text message states: "Visibility required". My heart drops as I see this because it means that he expects me to go to this client without my invisibility shield. This is a first for me since I was child.

Nervous, I grab my handbag and keys and jump into my old, beat-up blue Beetle, my precious Maisy, and follow my phone's directions down the highway. I don't know what I'm expecting—perhaps a dark den full of shifters smoking pot and snorting cocaine —but I find myself pulling into the circular driveway of a palace-sized mansion with an actual boom gate at the front complete with a security booth.

It reminds me of the place I used to call home as a child. But I shove that thought away as fast as it came.

Having been frequenting cage fighting dens for years now, I'm no stranger to brawny males flinging their animus around. I usually eighth-shield myself in the car park, however, and don't have to have contact with them when they can't see me.

So, with my heart pounding in my ears, I roll down my window as a smartly dressed man in a grey and black security uniform and a gun at his hip strolls up to me.

"Aurelia Naga?"

I swallow as his eyes survey me. "Aurelia Aquinas, actually."

It's animalia protocol that you take the surname

of whichever parent you take after—so I naturally took my mother's name.

He nods as if this suddenly makes more sense, and waves me through the boom gate.

Okay, so this Halfeather is possibly more loaded than my father. I briefly wonder if he is a dragon. They are rare—only a handful of families in our state—and they are always higher-up officials in the government or businessmen. I mean, who would say 'no' to a *dragon*? The threat there was permanent and assumed, so it only makes sense they get whatever they want and are able generate extreme wealth.

I find out immediately what order of animalia I'm dealing with as I drive through the boom gate, though the name should have given it away. The fountain in the middle of the circular drive is of a massive stone eagle, its wings poised as if about to take off in flight.

I personally think that arrogance of the bird shifting population is warranted. There is no greater pleasure in this world than flying. Soaring high above everything and letting the wind carry you? Honestly, everyone else *should* be envious.

But I'm no more comfortable knowing what type of beast this Halfeather is. Each order of animalia has their own genetic powers, and it just so happens that birds are the healing beasts of our kind.

If he is a wealthy eagle, that means he is probably related to, or best friends with, the top healers in the country. Whatever he needs, the fact that *I* am being called to help makes my skin crawl with anxiety.

Another security male, tall and in all black, guides me to park in a designated space next to a shining red Ferrari. I inwardly cringe, knowing full well I haven't washed Maisy in months and her faded blue paint is practically peeling. But on sight of the young male guard, my anima begins purring and preening inside of me alongside a bubbling nervousness. I clamp down on it because I need my head clear to deal with this.

The tall security guard, also an eagle by his dark blond spiked-up hair, gives me a handsome smile as I get out of my car. He gives me the usual, assessing once over unmated males give unmated females. Heat flares in my cheeks at his approving smile and I'm glad my shields hide the likely desire in my scent. I haven't had sex in over a year—a lone serpent who'd seen me at the shop, and *that* had ended badly. I really feel the absence of it in my life and an ache throbs deep within my stomach.

Once animalia hit puberty, we are taken to the

city's oracle, who is a member of the ancient House of Phoenix. They have the ability to see a person's soul-bound mates by the touch of a hand. When I'd gone at thirteen for my reading, the news had not been good. Another strike against me.

I had five mates. And two of them were already in jail.

If I'd thought my father had been furious about my anima, it was nothing compared to his furore when he'd found out how many and what orders my mates were. He'd gone back inside to the oracle to blackmail the names out of her. He told me that he didn't end up getting any of them, as it was a difficult skill for an oracle to perform.

It didn't matter because I had then been forbidden to speak of my mates to any living soul under any circumstances. To do so would lead me to disaster, father had said. If anyone knew who my mates were, everyone would know what *I* was right away. It would be a dead giveaway, and that information could not be out in the world. I would be stolen away by powerful beasts, chained up and used as a career breeder.

No one can know what I am.

That means I have to stay away from my mates

and do everything in my power to avoid them finding me.

I follow the security guy—Beak, he tells me his name is—as he leads me past the white Grecian pillars of the entrance into the mansion.

It's all gold and white marble inside, gilded portraits of birds on the walls and clinically clean. There's a small table off to the side where Beak puts on latex gloves and checks my battered black handbag. I shift with unease as he searches through it, pushing aside my case of tampons and compact mirror and opening my wallet to check my driver's license. Then he apologises as he confiscates the entire bag into a big safe behind his desk.

I raise my brows but say nothing as he leads me up the marble staircase, through a maze of red-carpeted corridors, and to a mahogany door. The entire time I stare at his ass and I let out a puff of air to try and let out some of the pressure building up in me. He glances back at me then, and I heat up like a wheat bag. Smirking, he smartly raps on the expensive wood, opens it, and leads me through.

"Aurelia Aquinas, Mr. Halfeather," he announces formally.

I gulp as I enter, feeling underdressed in my jeans and t-shirt combo as the wealthy male's office is revealed, dripping with all the expensive trimmings. Wood-panelled walls fitted with expensive oil paintings, gilded wall sconces, and a heavy mahogany desk. The room is big enough to hold a full lounge set, and everything matches in maroon leather.

What is *not* matching is a weaselly man coming around the desk, a sly smile curving his face.

My skin crawls at the pale, narrow-faced male and the brown eyes eagerly focused on me. He wears a long black robe like a medieval sorcerer, though he can't be older than fifty. His hair is black and receding and he gives off an observant, scummy sort of energy.

"Aurelia." He purrs my name with the familiarity of a doting uncle. "Thank you for coming."

I suppress a cringe as I try to give him a small smile. My father's *colleague.* I wonder what dark business they do together. "It's no problem."

"Your father tells me you are a talented healer."

I'm surprised my father has revealed to someone that he has a daughter. It's not like it's a huge secret, but he hides it when he can with non-court members. "Some might say that, yes, Mr. Halfeather."

His smile widens as I say his name. He's a man with an ego as big as his house, no doubt about it. But

I'm kicking myself because *who* would say I'm a 'talented healer'? I've been so isolated, no one, except my assessor during my healing course, knew me well enough to say that.

"Do you have any other powers?"

"No, sir." I lie.

He nods as if this confirms what he already knows. "I have a rather difficult situation that none of my healers have had much success with. I'm afraid you are my last effort at recovering this certain individual."

Ice slides down my spine at his clinical manner of speaking, at the fact that experienced, qualified healers have already tried to heal this person. Halfeather himself has probably also tried.

Is this a trap? A way for my father to teach me a lesson about trying to leave for college? I try not to appear nervous, but I think it still shows because Halfeather leans forward and speaks as if to a child. "Can you keep a secret, my sweet?"

I clear my throat. "I guess I can, Mr Halfeather."

"Just for me?"

"S-Sure."

Every instinct I possess tells me to run from this eagle. To leave and never look back and ring my father and blast him for sending me here. But they have my bag, they have my phone, and there is a bloody boom gate at the front.

There is no escaping.

He leads me from the room and a second security guard joins us from nowhere—another eagle, bulky, with dark brown hair and blonde tips. It seems Halfeather only trusts his own kind. It makes sense if he's doing shady business with people like my father.

Instead of taking me up the stairs, where I imagine the living areas are, we go *down*. One set of stairs and then another, and another. The elevators don't go down to wherever we're going. I know that because we pass two on our way.

We reach the end of a final set of stairs and Halfeather beams at me as we emerge into a dark room made of grey stone.

It's cold and barely lit with little lights on walls. I put my arms around myself, rubbing my gooseflesh and cursing my father's name. It looks more and more like the shady place I'd first expected. The entire thing is creepy, but I'm somehow drawn forward, wanting to know what the hell he's keeping down here. I've been privy to the secrets of many animalia, but no secret as grand as this one. Despite my rising panic, my feet move forward by some primal curiosity. Power is floating at the corners of my shields, but I do my best to ignore it.

We walk through one set of locked steel doors, and then a second set. Talk about secure.

"Here we are," Halfeather says brightly as the second set of doors swing open. "My pride and joy."

We stand before a cold, shadowy maw. There's stone set into the shape of a wide, low-ceilinged corridor that's long and dark enough that I can't see the end of it. Tiny lights are set at intervals along the walls, barely fighting away the shadowy gloom beyond. In between those intervals are steel bars. Cold realisation trickles down my spine.

Holy Mother...

Cells. This is a dungeon.

Chapter 4

Aurelia

S*hit.*

I stare around at my icy cold, stone-walled surroundings. The steel bars of the cages are like the bare incisors of a greedy animal, ready to gobble me whole.

Ahead, in the dark, something *shifts*. My insides turn into slush.

He's keeping people down here. Gods help me.

"It's not exactly *legal*," Halfeather says conspiratorially, his dark eyes gleaming with excitement.

"I dare say it's not." I smile sheepishly, as if I'm being coy. "Is this where you keep your debtors?"

He tuts at me in a casual manner that suggests he's thought about it before. "Hardly, my dear. Just the feral beasts who do me wrong. Cross me, as it were."

I try to hold myself together, at the same wondering how I could have been so stupid not to think my father's type of colleagues kept prisoners. *Of course* they do. They are all monsters like him.

"If you do this for me, my dear," Halfeather drawls, "you can consider your father's debt repaid in full."

My father's debt.

Fucking asshole! Rage bubbles through my veins, heady and hot as I realise my father is using me as his lackey. That to him, I am a valuable *thing* he can use over and over. That the likelihood of him actually letting me go for good is practically non-existent.

If this is what my life is going to be like until the end of time, I will *not* accept it.

I need a plan. I need to figure out how to get out of this. How to get out of my father's clutches. Merely crossing state lines to go to college isn't enough.

I have to maintain my composure here, with this powerful beast and his security. So, I act like I already know about the debt.

"Really?" I say, stopping our advance down the aisle to stare at him.

"Really," he replies with a wan smile.

I hesitate before saying, "I'd like that in writing, please."

His smile widens. "Clever girl, aren't you?" I bat my eyelashes in what I hope is a pretty manner, but I'm not sure because I haven't had much practice. It must work because he says, "I'll have my lawyer draw the papers up right this minute."

"You're so kind, Mr. Halfeather."

He makes a contented sound and sweeps me deep into the dungeon. Our four pairs of footsteps echo off the stone walls and I see hulking shadows lying in the cells we pass. We're surrounded by darkness when Halfeather stops in front of another steel door set between two cells.

"Just here is my prized possession. But he is consumed by a deathly illness of some kind that won't heal. Can you fix him, my little healer?"

I try to ignore the condescension in his voice as I look at the shadows about us uncertainly. I can barely see through the gloom and am more than certain that the large cells just feet away are all occupied with animalia.

"It is virtually impenetrable, my love," Halfeather says breezily, noting my nervous look at the other cells. "They cannot harm you, and they know better than to talk to you."

Talk to me!

Geez, he is far too comfortable in this dungeon, and it makes me think he enjoys coming down here. I look back at the steel door he's indicated. Unlike the others secured with bars, it looks like this inmate is in solitary confinement. There'd be no light in there at all.

My skin crawls at the thought of such mental torture. Asshole father or not, as a healer, I have the innate urge to help people, and that is something I won't fight my anima on. "How long has he been in there?" My voice is quiet, and I hope he finds it respectful. This is not a male I want to be on bad terms with.

Halfeather waves a dismissive hand. "You can do it, can you not? Your father assures me you are some... anomaly?"

"I suppose I am." I shrug. "I just think I have more patience than others." It's only half a lie.

"You can reach him through the door, yes?"

I close my eyes and send my awareness out towards the door, then through it. The thing is made of metal as thick as the length of my arm and I almost swear out loud. What kind of beast are they keeping in here that requires *this*? An animalia in human form lies on the floor, unmoving but breathing. I can't register the order he is, which is odd in of itself.

"I can get through," I confirm.

He turns on his heel. "Simply knock on the door when you are done." He strides away as if business is finished, the two security males following him.

My heart sinks into my nether regions. "You're going to leave me here?"

His voice gets further and further away. "As I say, it's quite secure. Beak and Scuff will be down to check on you."

I swallow. What choice do I have here? "Right. Okay."

The boom of the steel door shutting echoes down the passageway like a prophecy of doom. Okay, so that's a bit dramatic, I know, but I'm in a real, live, literal dungeon. I can't help but feel I'm being made a prisoner, too. Halfeather's message is clear to me. I *have* to do this.

I stand in the gloom for a moment, my skin crawling, my heart pounding, feeling all the resentment in the world for my scum of a father. I really should just focus—

A masculine voice reaches out to me like midnight silk. "You can't help him."

I freeze like a deer, straining my ears, not daring to breathe. The voice comes from the cell next to the steel door and I'm close enough to look inside, but I can't make anything out. The voice says nothing further and heavy chains slide across the floor. Gulping, I slowly swivel my head to look into the cell on my right. I adjust my eyes by pulling my eagle form into them, and even with that, I can only just make out a man-shaped figure in the middle of the cell.

I look behind me, and with relief, I see a stone wall—I won't have my back to one of the prisoners. But on either side of that wall are two occupied cells.

Cloaked in darkness, the prisoners are nothing but menacing shadows, and that makes the whole thing worse.

But I know where the voice came from, so I look again to the cell to the left of the steel door.

I clear my throat. "Why do you say that?"

Chains clink as if he's moving closer to the bars. "None of the healers could do anything and they were all a lot more experienced than you."

I know two things from his voice. One, that he is *not* rabid because those beasts don't talk in proper sentences, and two, he's had some sort of education by the confident way his mouth moves around his words.

Animalia criminals deserving of a dungeon usually aren't the school-going sort.

But that arrogant voice, that condescending tone cuts into me and I know then that I will fix the beast behind the steel door, even if it kills me. Do I have an ego? Maybe. I suppose this means I do. Perhaps a lifetime of being shunned by my own family has made me into someone who scrambles to achieve *something* with her life. And every healing I do is an achievement. A success.

And some arrogant male questioning my ability is the single most irritating thing to me right now.

I level a look in his general direction. "Interesting. I suppose we'll see."

The figure of the beast who'd spoken shifts, and he leans further forward, pushing himself between the bars and into the field of the meagre light.

My breath catches in my throat as a face of wolfish, masculine beauty comes into view. Oh, he's a wolf, no doubt about it. He has wavy black hair and scruff on his jaw, but neither of those things are what gives him away. No, it's the devilish, white-toothed smile and a rogue gleam in his eye that promises *trouble*. Metal glints and I know he wears a stud on his ear.

He licks his lips and I can't help but zone in on

the movement. When he speaks again, his voice is heavy with flirtation, and he cocks his head playfully. "What is your name, princess?"

"You're not supposed to be talking to me," I say, forcing myself to look away.

A second voice, from the cell behind me and opposite the wolf's, drawls in a slow voice like molten fire made into sound. "There are no cameras." Then his voice takes on a deeper, colder cadence. "There's no one to see what goes on down here."

Chapter 5

Aurelia

A chill trickles down my spine at the fiery menace in that voice, like the deep parts of a volcano. I have no idea what to say to a barely concealed threat like that, so I simply turn around and decide ignoring these beasts is best. I check my shields, knowing full well I can withstand any attack that is thrown at me. But if I'm correct, that heinous twang I feel in the air hovering around the cells is a magical dampener—and a very expensive one. So, without fear but a lot of alertness, I hone back onto the male behind the steel door.

What manner of illness does he have?

I feel gross for invading his body without consent, but with an unconscious patient, I don't have a choice. I quickly scan his insides, intending on sweeping my magic from his crown to his toes, but I stop short at his neck. My heart beats irregularly as I recognise what it is.

Why my father specifically sent me to heal this male.

A darkness clings to his spine, curling around his spinal cord as if it wants to choke the life out of him and his animus. It's an actual snake of shadow and malice, his jaws set around the base of the male's skull. Very similar to the way my father had me pinned by his snake's jaw just an hour ago, except I've never seen a shadow snake coiled *inside* a person's body.

It is dark magic, typical of serpents, and I have no doubt in my mind that this is a magical disease brought on by contact with dark magic.

I wonder if my father did this. He's capable of it, and I know in my heart that if anyone could figure out this illness, it's him.

Then why send me here to undo it? No, this has to be someone else's work. Someone just as dark and cold.

Being so entangled with his spine, I'm going to have to remove it one bloody inch at a time, prising it away slowly to ensure his spinal cord is left intact. No wonder the other healers left him for dead. *Any* mark on his spine and he will be left with permanent paralysis that no run-of-the-mill healer could fix.

It will require meticulous and painstaking work, hours of slow focus, and I'd be lying if the thought of such a task doesn't excite me just a little. Maybe I'm insane, but this is why my father considers me his best healer. This is real complex work, and it makes me feel like there's a reason for why I was born.

I take up a seat, cross-legged on the dungeon floor, the cold tile seeping into my ass uncomfortably. I pull my cardigan off as I'm going to generate heat from all the work.

A low whistle sounds behind me, from a different cell than the last prisoners who'd spoken. I try not to let it bother me. I'm not here for them. They're not my patient and are therefore unimportant.

I work for an hour, beginning right at the male's tailbone, persuading the shadow snake to uncurl himself with tiny, precise manoeuvres of my power. I'm sweating within minutes, and it almost feels like no time at all when I hear the distant slam of the dungeon door and the heavy booted steps of the guards.

Disentangling myself from my patient, I open my eyes to see the two eagle males staring down at me.

I groan, cracking my neck as they frown at me sitting on the dungeon floor. My hormones must be raging because before I can even think about it, I raise my hand in a silent question for help. Beak is nice enough to offer his back. I grasp it and am silently shocked by the warmth of his large male hand. I know exactly how long it's been since I've even *touched* a male with my skin. Even a female. Accepting and giving people change at work is the only way I get people contact, but even so, most people make EFT purchases these days.

Even without the power usage from the hour of healing, I'm more thirsty than any regular female anima, and am wet just from the touch of this fertile male.

I might not be able to hunt down my mates and bed them, but my anima *desperately* wants to do *something*.

Beak doesn't scent my desire, though. My shield is titanium and has been that way since the day at the oracle. I cannot let any male scent me, because within seconds they'll know I'm no common eagle.

My fingers leave Beak's hand oh so reluctantly

and I'm ashamed that he notices, a mildly hungry look flashing across his face. He seems to struggle with it for a moment as I put on my jacket and follow the two of them down the corridor. Beak looks back at me once and his companion grunts something at him I don't hear. One downside to my seven shields is that it stifles my hearing a little. But I do see Beak shake himself and become a professional once again. I get a tiny bit of giddy satisfaction from this interaction just before a pang of sadness hits me.

I'm destined for a life of *this*. If I can't let males scent me, I will be a single anima for the rest of my life. I'll die with both my honour and my secret intact, but *god,* sometimes honour seems overrated.

I stare at both fine guards' asses all the way to Mr. Halfeather's office, my eyes half lidded, my fingers twitching, telling myself it's just the healing exertion having me look for a boost and not desperation for real, skin-to-skin company.

The old eagle is sitting at his desk as I walk past the two guards towards him.

"I'll need to return daily," I say softly, "until it's all out. Shouldn't take more than a week."

"A full week?" he asks with raised brows. I feel his eagle's vision take in every one of my sweating pores.

I grimace, wondering when I last exfoliated. "It's a persistent...illness that requires tedious work. I don't think anyone else would have the patience for it, honestly."

Thinking he'd be annoyed by the delay, I'm surprised when a slow smile spreads across his face. "Well, I can't complain if I get to see you every day now, can I?"

I drive away from Halfeather's mansion, trying not to think about the way Beak pulled open my car door for me. It had been a feat of willpower not to let down a shield, stand on my tiptoes and sniff him properly.

How I wished he'd slipped his number into my handbag, but he hadn't—I'd checked twice. The desperation was probably written all over me and he'd likely been put off by it.

Pondering on what a not-desperate female looks like, I do something I usually avoid and stop to get drive-thru takeaway, wolfing down an entire burger, fries and shake meal. I feel a little better afterwards, so once I get home and shower again, I decide to get ready for work.

My eyelids droop a little from tiredness, but I don't want to mope around thinking about what happened with my father here at home and then spending my morning literally locked in a dungeon and then again lusting over Beak, fine as he'd been. I need to keep myself busy. Sometimes my aunt gives me a bonus if I work overtime. My goal is to make as much money as I can before college starts, when I'll have to purchase ridiculously expensive books and accommodation.

My meagre allowance isn't going to cut it and there is no way my father is going to pay for any of my college things. I am financially on my own.

My mother would not have wanted this for me. I'd never known her as she'd died when I was five, but in my head, she loved me more than anything else in the world. I held onto that thought like it was a life raft, and on my first nights living alone, that's exactly what it had been.

When I reach work, a moderately sized grocery and convenience store, Aunt Charlotte looks up from where she's filing her nails, fluffs up her bleached blonde curls and looks me up and down with a disapproving frown.

Some things never change.

Nothing is more important to my father than his family, and he's looked after his sister since they were young. Always giving her money for Louboutins and Prada handbags whenever she batted her overlong eyelash extensions at him.

"What are you doing here?" she says through shiny red lips. "Mace said—"

"I'll be working for him during the mornings this week, so I thought I might as well help out here until close. You'll be home to have dinner with the kids that way."

Charlotte was a regina to two mates. Uncle Ben works in the mines, fly in fly out style, and Uncle Ron is a plumber. They are all sworn snakes to my father's court and hence avoid me like the plague. Ben is the nicer of the two, probably because he isn't here enough to see the political nightmare I am. When I first moved out to the bungalow at the back of their house, he would bring me leftover dinners, often sneaking a piece of chocolate or two wrapped in a napkin.

I'm pretty sure my father uses this store for money laundering or worse, but I'm not allowed in the back office, so I can't be sure.

Aunt Charlotte looks down her nose at me and

nods stiffly. I thought that me leaving for college at summer's end would cheer her up, but she's as snub-nosed as ever. But I understand her because I'd *been* her once and you don't understand your privilege until it's taken away.

Chapter 6

Aurelia

The next day, I roll out of bed, chug two mugs of coffee and head back out to Halfeather's mansion.

So what that I wear my nice pair of skinny jeans and a blouse that shows a teensy bit of cleavage?

A girl can dream.

When you've lived by yourself, in isolation as long as I have, that's all you have. Your imagination and your dreams. And I'd say I'm pretty proficient at using both—perhaps it's the only reason I'm still sane.

I'm greeted in much the same manner as yesterday, except Halfeather snatches up my hand and kisses it delicately, as if I'm something precious.

My stomach clenches at the royal treatment, wondering if there's anything ulterior behind it. But I stick a smile on my face as if I enjoy it and he releases me to my guards. Beak and Scuff have easy smiles today and I don't fight the racing of my heart when I smile back.

It takes me and entire two flights of steps to gather enough courage to ask Beak, "So, is this your permanent gig?"

"Sort of." He scratches the back of his head, one huge, tanned bicep flexing. My eyes follow the movement and he grins at me. I tear my gaze away, realising he's showing me his body on purpose. Bloody eagles and their peacocking, I swear he's going to be the end of me. "We go to college in a couple of week," he continues, leading me down to the dungeon. "This is just a summer job for us."

"Sweet." I nod. "Which college?"

But he's opened the final set of doors and ushers me in. I quickly ask, "Hey, um, are there any lights in there?" I rub my arms against the cold. "It's ridiculously dark and I practically can't see where I'm walking."

Beak and Scuff shift uncomfortably as they escort me past the first lot of cells. "Mr. Halfeather likes it dark down here," Scuff says.

"Maybe just for the hour I'm here?" I bat my eyelashes at Beak, trying to channel my inner, sexy, helpless, Aunt Charlotte. They exchange a look. I whisper to appeal to their subconscious male animus. "Just a little bit?"

My cooing wins in the end. "Just a bit," Beak says kindly.

I grin at them before they head out and inevitably shut the massive steel door. Somehow, it actually worked, and I wonder what else I can get away with by channeling Aunt Charlotte.

Alone once again in the gloom, with nothing but predators shifting around me, chains clanking, I wait there until the lights come on. A gentle silver glow comes to life around me. It's hardly better, but now I can actually make out the colour of the dull grey stone brick beside my patient's steel door.

A low, rough chuckle skulks through the air, sending my hackles rising. It's not a laugh of amusement or joy, it's sheer nastiness.

"Scared of the dark?" someone jeers from behind me.

Animalia males pounce on fear, some of them even enjoy provoking it, their animus wanting to hunt prey. The idea that I'm acting like prey has me gritting my teeth.

"I fear nothing," I say into the shadows. "Least of all some animalia stupid enough to get locked up in here."

The man in the cell to the right of my patient's door is sitting on a steel chair. It's pushed as far back into the cell as possible, so the light only reaches his bare, tattooed thighs, telling me that he's naked. He's tall and no more than a shadow, his hands tied behind his back.

I wonder how he pees.

He doesn't speak, but the male in the cell opposite him and behind me says in a leering voice, "Show us your pussy, girly. I bet it's real sweet."

Okay, so I'm regretting my choice of nicer clothing as my nose wrinkles in disgust.

Before he can say any more, a voice growls from my other side. "Get away from him, princess. He's a dirty bastard."

I recognise the wolf's voice. Because I'm not entirely stupid, I do listen to him and position myself closer to my patient's door.

The wolf is there, in the cell directly to my left, and pushes his face through the bars to look at me.

Did I think Beak was handsome just before? Because by all the wild gods, every cell in my body rears their little molecular heads to register the sheer masculine beauty of the wolf's face.

A face that is currently hungrily fixed on me.

I'm glad I'm not the only desperate animalia around, but I doubt this male lacks women in his life when he's not chained up. Women probably fall on their knees begging and panting wherever he goes.

I frown, more at myself than anything, and he shows me a row of straight white teeth. "So you'll flirt with the dicky birds, but not with me?" he asks coyly.

My heart skips a beat and I remind myself to keep my breathing even. He might not be able to scent me, but wolves are more socially aware of body language than the rest.

I eye him for a moment, getting a better look at him in the new light. There's dirt smeared on a bare muscular torso so ripped I know at once he's been bred for fighting. I've been to enough illegal fights to know the feral, bloodthirsty, I-eat-beasts-for-fun look. I wonder when he's last had a shower as I note the sheen of sweat glistening over the wolf tattoo spanning his muscular chest. I can clearly see now that his earring is a black stud, a gem of some sort. His smile widens as it becomes very obvious that I'm checking him out, so I turn my head away from him in arrogant dismissal.

Clearly my anima takes over because even without looking at him, I'm flirting back. "Beak's got big muscles," I say, pushing my ponytail over my shoulder. "What do you have?"

From my periphery, he scoffs, then pouts. "I have pretty eyes, though, don't you think?"

I don't look at him as I sit down in my cross-legged position. "Yeah, they're alright, I suppose."

He gasps in mock offence, and I have to refrain from grinning outright. This is all because of my dud of a vibrator from yesterday. I *knew* I should have broken into my savings to get a new one. My own fingers only did so much with an appetite like mine and I can't very well be flirting with the prisoners. I blink at the steel door, wondering what the wolf has done to displease Halfeather enough to land himself here.

"Give me ten seconds with Beak," comes that angry molten voice in the cell opposite the wolf's. "And I'll fuck him to high hell."

"You'll fuck him?" the wolf jeers. "With your big dragon dick? He'll be sore for days."

There's a bloody dragon in here too?! Why hasn't his rich daddy pulled him out?

But the dragon drawls, "Not with my dick, you idiot. With my claws. His pretty face won't be a face anymore."

"I'd take him out in two seconds," the wolf says, sighing as if thinking about a wonderful fantasy. "What I'd give for *two* seconds."

Animalia males measure dicks whenever they get together like this. Especially when females are about. I suppose they haven't been around females in a while if they're peacocking for *me* right now.

I can't help thinking that, whatever they've done, this whole thing is wrong. And leaving them without proper hygiene? Or clothes? It's inhumane. I've seen feral animalia treat their subordinates better in their forest communes.

I sigh and glance at the wolf still standing at the bars, staring down at me. Both males have quieted their bickering.

My anima is moving my mouth for me because I'm mad enough to ask in a low voice, "What's your name?"

He grins, his eyes brightening. They're hazel, I note, a swirl of delicious greens and browns that remind me of dangerous, ancient forests and they beckon to me with the call of a wild song. But he ruins it and says, "You show me yours and I'll show you mine."

I roll my eyes, scoffing at his choice of wording and turn away back to my charge behind the door. I have one hour and I need to get as much done as I can. I close my eyes.

"Savage," he blurts out. "My name is Savage."

Chapter 7

Savage

The moment this woman stumbled into my dungeon like some angel floating through the gates of heaven, I'd thought I was hallucinating. Or dying.

Lightning had buzzed all around me, waking me up, and all at once I'd felt a hurricane of desire flood my veins. I had wanted to run my fingers through all that long silky raven hair, touch her cheek and see how soft it was. I had wanted to pull her into my cage and bury my nose between her legs.

I had also wanted to rip out Halfeather's throat for standing so close to her. And today, she'd come in with Beaky and Scuffy, all flirty and smiley, and I vowed to tear out their feathers and wear them as a coat.

I forget all of that right now as she glances at me again with those long, dark lashes fluttering over impossibly blue eyes and I feel something stir deep inside my cock.

Understandable, since I've not been in contact with a woman for a gods damned long time.

"Lia," she says quietly, as though she's wondering why she's telling me at all.

Ah, me and my charms loosened her tongue sure enough. It was only a matter of time.

"Lia." I taste her name, sounding out the letters and wondering how they would sound in a moan as I came inside of her. "What's it short for?"

She hesitates, but gives it to me because she can't resist. "Aurelia."

Perfect. Pretty. Angelic. A name I could get tattooed where everyone could see it.

It's also a unique name. I'd have no trouble finding her once I get out of here. She turns away from me once again and I lick my lips at her stunning side profile, wanting her to show me her blue ocean eyes again. I can't see him, but Scythe growls at me softly from the cell on Lia's other side—a warning.

My brother knows me, of course. Knows that it's dangerous for me to pursue a woman like this. He's probably trying to protect her—he's always trying to save the world from me and my dirty paws. So I settle down and watch Lia start up her healing magic on the boogeyman in solitary. He'd already been here when we'd arrived and I'd known that whoever he was, he was a part of our mating group right away. Even Halfeather's shields can't mask the ancient bond between us—a gold thread that links our animus' through space and eternity. But we'd not found our regina yet, our centre, and that was exactly what had gotten us into this fuck up of a situation.

I sit down on the stone, mirroring Aurelia—Lia, as she liked to be called. But I think I'm going to stick with 'Princess'. It matches her delicate features, her haughty, sweet nose in the air, and her I'm-not-scared-of-the-big-bad-wolf personality. She walks a little like a princess too, and I can't take my eyes off her every time she walks up to me.

Every time? Dear Mother Wolf, I'm delusional. I've seen her walk all of *two* times. Who cares, though? I'd known I wanted to take a bite out of those hips the moment I'd seen her. Not an actual bite, more of a mouthful, more of a 'let me lick you all over and see if you taste as good as you look.'

The magic dampener on my cell refrains me from feeling her out properly as she closes her eyes and broaches the bogeyman's steel door with her magic. It's such a shame because I'm fucking desperate to scent her and I just know it's going to be spectacular when I do.

I glance back at Xander, opposite me. He usually has his eyes closed, listening to whatever European rock music or Mongolian throat singing he has on his device. When we'd first arrived, he'd raged for a full week straight in his cell, almost tearing the place down, driving the rest of us mad until the guards had given in and let him have his music. The fucking old beaker didn't want to drive us rabid, which I took to mean he wanted us sane for *something*.

Xander is frowning at Aurelia through his old scars. He can't use his damaged eyes without his power and that's left him agitated—and creepy looking, because they're black hollows from where they'd dug them out with their bare claws when he was a kid. I turn back to look at Lia. It's pretty impressive that she can sit there for a full hour and fix the beast next door. I don't think I've ever seen anyone hold power or concentration for that long.

We sit and watch her—well, Xander listens—while Scythe remains still in his cage, which is the best anyone can ask of him. I lean my forehead against the bars of my cell, my stomach grumbling. They feed us whenever they feel like it, which is not often. Fair punishment, I suppose, for what we'd done. I don't care though, I'd do it all over again given the chance, and I know the others would say the same. Xander enjoys a good slaughter even more than Scythe and me, and that's saying something.

Chapter 8

Aurelia

I'm quite happy about the progress I've made today with the shadow snake. I still can't tell what type of animus the male has, but it doesn't affect my ability to heal him. I report back to Mr. Halfeather when Beak and Scuff come to get me. He never asks me details about the illness or the manner of it, and I vaguely wonder if this is some weird thing my father is doing to test me. But none of that makes sense, given my father already knows what I'm capable of.

Whatever I did for the animalia behind that steel door, I was acutely aware of the three prisoners I'd seen a little more of today—and the fourth, a hyena, I think, who'd spoken so crassly to me. There were other creatures in that dungeon—I had seen them as

I walked past their cages on the way back. They were all slumped on the cement floor with their backs turned towards me as if they were half alive. The only ones who seemed to be interested in what went on were the sleaze bag and the wolf, *Savage*.

The name given from a fighting family, if I've ever heard one. Wolves are notorious for underground fighting rings. It's a good way to make money if you're good at it. High risk, high reward, and with that expensive gem on his ear, I bet he did real well at his job.

I leave Halfeather's manor with Beak opening the door of my Beetle for me once again. Chivalry isn't dead, and it makes my beast of an anima preen and coo at him.

"Thanks." I only let myself smile at him as I get into my car.

"Will I see you at the Academy in two weeks?" he asks.

I choke. "You're going to *Animus* Academy?"

He runs a hand through his hair, smirking. "Yeah, I got the order a few weeks ago. My parents were so relieved."

Males seem to think it's a flex being ordered to attend the college we send our most volatile, promiscuous and errant new adults. The idea is to temper and civilise them before they hit the workforce and wider community, so they won't be such a menace to the fearful human population we try to live alongside. Naturally, once you receive the order to attend, you *have* to go, otherwise they hunt you down and take you kicking and screaming bound in tourmaline chains. Beak seems pretty controlled, but there must be a feral hunter under that pretty face.

Why he thinks *I'm* going there is beyond me.

"Do I look like I need to go there?" I ask in horror.

He smiles sheepishly. "Well, I thought because of your power, you'd be... no? Well, good for you then."

I leave the mansion, heading to my favourite fast-food drive-thru before I'm due at work. The entire way, Savage's face presses in on my mind's eye. Seeing these beasts behind bars in such conditions, slumped against the wall, dirty and one even without clothes, makes me cringe. There is no humanity in it at all. When I head into work, a discounted stack of sweatpants catches my eye and the whisper of a wild thought runs through my mind.

It's the morning of the third day of my visits to Halfeather's dungeon and I feel the edges of fatigue creeping in. My power is sizeable, but the strain of both maintaining my seven shields and being around these males has me feeling some kind of way.

But I find that a bubble of eagerness engulfs me. I'm likely finally going mad, but I actually look forward to it. It's almost like going to a real job where I have regular faces grinning at me upon my entry. I'm wanted here. Beak and Scuff shoot me flirty smiles and Beak even hands me a few Hershey's Kisses from the frosted glass bowl he keeps at his desk.

"You deserve it," he says, grinning.

Be still my fluttering heart! I blush and keep my mouth shut in case I say something dumb like, 'What time do you get off?'

A part of me shakes its head in dismay, but a reasonable part of me googled it last night and I know it has a name: Touch deprivation.

Even in Aunt Charlotte's shop I'm usually relegated to stacking shelves and cleaning, my contact with clients is limited to the occasional cashier coverage when Charlotte goes to the bathroom to fix her makeup.

My father took me out of school once he moved

me out of home. I've been homeschooled since then, using an online system one of the high school teachers in his court had set up. It was lonely, so I ended up sneaking to the local Salvation Army store, picking up as many books as I could manage after I shopped for clothes. If I couldn't be a part of the real world, my fictional book worlds were always waiting for me along with my fictional friends.

No one except Uncle Ben has given me chocolate or anything remotely resembling a gift since I was a kid.

So I *know* I'm a complete loony as I'm heading down into a dungeon of darkness with a group of apex predators and my anima purrs with glee. My lips twitch with a faint smile as Beak opens the second steel door.

I waltz in with the Hershey's Kisses in my hand and, this time even the creepy cold can't affect my good mood. Beak shakes his head in amusement as I pass him. He probably thinks I'm mental, and I doubt he's all that wrong. They've put the lights on for me already, and it's slightly brighter than yesterday. Making a surprised noise at the back of my throat at Beak's further kindness, I stride down.

It's like my body knows Savage is waiting for me because I immediately forget about Beak's lingering gaze and clench in anticipation of those wolfish hazel eyes. I'm walking past the leering male's cage, stiffening in case I get another lewd comment, but as I glance inside his cell, I stop dead in my tracks.

Dear Wild Mother.

Lying on the stones of his cell is a hyena, clearly having shifted into his animus form before his head was separated from his body. There's a pool of blood between the two parts and my stomach gives a fell lurch. One of my hands finds my mouth, covering it as if I can also cover the scene of the murder from my mind.

"*Lee-ah.*" Savage sings my name in the cadence of a happy children's song.

Chains scrape, a body shifts, but I ignore him and turn, forcing my eyes to the cell opposite of the hyena's, where the naked male is still sitting on his metal chair. I can see a little more of him today. He's a big beast, a late-twenties animalia covered in black tattoos from his feet to his neck. But one tattoo stands out: five fine lines of ancient text on the left side of his neck. This and two other signs tell me what his animus is. Ice-blue eyes glint at me through the dark. Long, silver hair that brushes his shoulders stands out amidst the gloom. On the left side of his neck are five lines of text representing five gill slits. He's a shark.

He's still. So still as he looks at me, powerful chest taking slow, deep breaths, large biceps pushed out from where his arms are tied behind his back. In my woeful life healing all sorts of dark creatures, I'd yet to meet a shark—and for good reason. Most of them go mad on land, the theory being that they were never meant to leave their marine home. Indeed, almost all marine animalia choose to live out their lives in deep parts of the ocean in converted form, never turning human ever again.

So what the hell is this one doing here?

Chapter 9

Aurelia

"Princess, get away from my brother." Savage's deep voice cuts through the spell the shark has on me and I shake myself before moving away to the steel door my patient lies behind. Savage pushes his head through the bars of his cell. He's sitting down already, but there are bags under his eyes that make him look even more dangerous. He gives me a sort of deranged smile that makes my stomach flop.

"What happened to the hyena?" I ask quietly.

A low, dark laugh, like a rumbling volcano, comes from the dragon in the cell behind me. "It got what was coming to it."

I turn to look at the dragon, feeling Savage watch

my every move. I can't see much of the male except to note that he, too, is chained, but not to a chair like the shark. Instead, both his arms are stretched out, chains binding him to the walls on either side. Barbaric; his arms must hurt so much.

I can't make out his face, where the light doesn't reach, but I can see he has black jeans on the bottom half of a typical dragon male's body.

Cut from stone, lean, shredded muscle that's puckered with scars, old and new. He has a piercing on one nipple and, in typical dragon style, long black hair cascading down his defined pecs. But the thing most interesting about him is the pair of white headphone cords leading up to his ears. A device is hooked into the waistband of his jeans.

"Checking me out, hatchling?" the dragon rumbles. His voice is cold and monotone.

I jump, pulling myself out of a thirsty haze and hope my face isn't sheepish. "Sorry. Don't your arms hurt?"

I get the impression he's glaring at me through the bars, but Savage snorts from behind me. "My brother is a little bloodthirsty shark. He took care of the hyena, princess. You don't have to worry about him talking shit to you anymore."

My heart leaps into my throat as I whirl back around. "What?" I exclaim. "How did he— When— What?!"

Savage smirks, looking me up and down, and I heat up immediately. Even slumped against the bars of his cell, he looks capable of jumping up at a minute's notice and tearing somebody's throat out. But the shark in the other cell couldn't have gotten to the hyena in the cell *opposite* him, surely.

I don't know what is more confusing. The fact that he'd managed it, or the fact that he'd done it out of some chivalry.

"Don't you worry your pretty little head about it," Savage says.

I scowl at the condescension in his voice and then stop short of a retort. "Wait, did you say *brother*?" I frown at Savage.

He doesn't take his eyes off me. "Mmm."

"But he's a—"

"Our father was the rex of two females. One wolf, one shark."

While it isn't uncommon to have a mating group with different orders, a marine in a soul-bond with land animalia *is* incredibly rare and unfortunate since they could never all be truly together for their whole lives. But this is also the very reason I can't reveal my mating group to anyone—*all* five of my mates are males of different animus orders. It's more than strange—it should be impossible.

I promptly decide that's enough interacting with the prisoners for today and sit down in my usual spot in front of the steel door. Before I start, I glance behind me at the dragon.

"Why does he have headphones in?" I ask Savage quietly.

"Do you know where the term 'berserk' comes from, princess?" he asks, looking at his fingernails.

I shake my head, wondering where this is going.

"It comes from the people known as the Berserkers of old Northern Europe. They were like Vikings, a fighting and pillaging sort of lifestyle. But these people would run into battle and go into a trance-like state where they'd kill anything and anyone in their path. Including each other. So, Xander is kinda like that. Without his music, he goes nuts and tries to kill everyone."

I raise my brows and glance over my shoulder again, where I'm sure the dragon, Xander, is listening. But he remains silent in his cell.

That explains why they'd allowed the music, but

the thought of a beast *needing* such a thing to control himself speaks volumes about the kind of life he's had. Dragons are brutal beasts, but usually their youth are extremely well cared for.

Savage smiles at me as if he hasn't just told me two completely murderous things in the last five minutes. I've never been on the receiving end of a smile like *this* before. Not since I was child. It's genuine, doting, almost honest, and it makes my heart do funny, unwelcome things.

I can't help but return it. His eyes flick down to my lips, and I take a deep breath to calm my raging anima.

"Oh." I remember, looking down at my hand. "Do you want some chocolate, Savage?"

"Mmm, say my name one more time."

I glance back up at him in surprise, but he's got his eyes closed. I take the opportunity to stare at his perfect, rugged face. The apex of my thighs is *throbbing*.

Clearing my throat, I say, "It's um... a Hershey's Kiss."

His eyes fly open, his hazel eyes no more than blown out, dilated pupils. "Yes, Lia, I'll take a kiss from you."

I sincerely hope there really isn't any surveillance on his dungeon like Xander told me that first day because I lean forward, going on my knees, and pass him the small, foil-wrapped chocolate. I'm careful to give it to him without our fingers touching.

"Do they feed you?" I ask, glancing at Xander behind me.

"Sometimes." With his big fingers, Savage unwraps the foil delicately, corner by corner, as if he's trying to stretch out the pleasure of opening it. I stare at him for a moment before I look back at the dragon.

I'm nervous to ask but, hell, you only live once, right? And these males seem like they could use a bit of kindness. "I can put this in your mouth if you like, um... Xander?"

The dragon is silent for a moment, before he says as if it's a challenge, "Go on then, hatchling, how good is your aim?"

Blushing at the term of endearment used for winged children, I don't tell him that my aim is not good at all. I get to my feet, unwrap the second chocolate from its foil and re-wrap it in one of my speciality shields.

I'm powerful at my secondary power, healing, but I'm even *better* at shields.

I make a show of tossing the chocolate towards Xander's mouth, but in reality, I just levitate it really fast towards him. He shifts a little to catch it, but it finds its mark. Once the chocolate is in his mouth, he goes still. Apex predator still.

And I know he's sensed the bubble shield I had around the chocolate.

He thinks I'm an eagle because of my healing powers. This is the narrative we've been weaving my whole life. I shouldn't have this extra magic like I do. It's not a known power to *any* animalia order.

It was a stupid, stupid risk, but he *is* a prisoner. Who's he going to tell? And who would believe him?

Hastily, I shuffle away, and to my relief, he doesn't say anything. The third chocolate is in my hand and I glance back at Savage. The wolf is concentrating deeply on his chocolate and I see that he's only taken teeny bites from the corners.

My heart pangs in sadness a little.

"Will your brother take one, do you think?"

"Who, Scythe?" he says, eyes darting down the dungeon. "Nah, he only eats raw fish these days."

"Ah, right."

So the shark is a little more than feral. I sit down to start my work, goosebumps puckering my skin as I remember those ice-blue eyes sitting just feet from me.

When I leave with Beak and Scuff after my healing session, I'm surprised by the heaviness I feel at leaving the prisoners behind me. I vaguely wonder if this is how people feel when they part with their friends.

Chapter 10

Aurelia

I *know* I'm delusional in thinking the prisoners in the dungeon are my friends. I'm a complete idiot for playing happy families with them —*sharing* things, *smiling* and getting a fluttery heart. Except I don't have anyone else in my life and is it so bad if I have an alright time chatting to them briefly? Is it so bad if Savage's and Beak's attention brightens my day just a little bit?

It's pathetic, I know. They're dangerous males. *And* they're prisoners.

So the next day, even if one part of me is screaming not to do it, that the risk is too great and I'll get into trouble, I'm going to do something stupid and I'm not even thinking about the consequences.

It's so unlike me that I can't even comprehend it.

I find myself walking into Halfeather's mansion with one of my strongest shields hiding a folded pair of discounted XL black track pants tucked under my arm. I hold my breath as Beak opens my car door, his usual flirty smile on his face as he takes my bag.

Suddenly, I'm not surprised he's been ordered to Animus Academy. His eyes are telling me that he wants to fuck. Promiscuity amongst our males is an issue. STDs for one thing, inter-court politics for another. It leads to more bloodshed than it's worth. Oddly, my anima isn't rearing up and wanting to grab at him like I expect. Am I getting used to the attention?

Of course, with my entire life being a study in shielding, I get the pants into the dungeons without a hitch. Getting the pants into Scythe's cell will be another thing entirely. It will also give away my power.

So it looks like I'm a risk taker now, but here I am faced with something I've never come across before. The primitive female anima within me appreciates that Scythe has *killed* a male for me.

I'd like to think they'd already had some sort of beef. That I'm not the only reason Scythe wanted that hyena dead. Whatever my brain thought, my anima wanted to thank the shark for such a display of blatant protection.

Perhaps the ferality of the prisoners is rubbing off on me because it seems like I'm letting my anima take control more and more by the day. Maybe Beak is right about me needing to go to Animus Academy after all.

Beak and Scuff lead me down to the dungeons once again, slamming the door shut behind me, but that ominous sound can't make me flinch today.

"Lia?" Savage's voice is a beacon in the gloom and a balm for any nervousness I feel.

"Hi, it's me." My voice sounds tiny compared to his.

I stride quickly past the cells, trying not to let my eagerness show. When I pass the hyena's cell, the body and head have been removed, and the scent of bleach even passes through my shields. I wonder what Halfeather does with the bodies of his prisoners.

The scent of fresh blood is also coming out loud and strong from the shark's cell. Yesterday, Savage said his brother's name was Scythe—another fighting name. Nervously, I step before him.

Ice-cold eyes like the dark depths of the Mariana

Trench shine through the gloom. *Danger,* my anima warns. *This one is a killer.*

I swallow as I reach out with my power and assess his body for the injuries I can smell. The shark doesn't show any response to my magic brushing against him. He simply sits there leaning against the back of the chair, eyes on me like cold, cold pokers. I can tell that his shoulder's been dislocated and that he or someone else has relocated it back into the socket—the tendons are all inflamed and a little mangled. There is also a break in his humerus, already healing due to his natural animus magic. But because of the magical dampeners on the dungeon, the process is slower than expected. I speed up the healing and seal the fracture shut.

He's silent throughout the whole thing. Usually, I get a grunt or something from the repair of a broken bone, but Scythe just sits there as if it doesn't bother him, watching me with the kind of precision I imagine only a shark can muster.

Healing is instinctual for me. It's hard for my power to see someone in pain and not do anything about it. It goes against literally everything that I am in my core, not to heal. But I suddenly realise that I never asked for his permission.

An icky feeling crawls through me and I mutter, "I'm sorry, I should have asked."

He says nothing.

I can't help but feel his injuries are a consequence of what he did to the hyena. What he did out of revenge for me. I wonder what he's thinking. What desire he had to kill the animalia and how the hell he'd done it.

The track pants at my side burn like contraband. I paid for them fair and square and now it seems even more imperative to give this male a gift.

Will he take it? There is no kindness coming off him, nothing close to human connection. I get the urge to turn away from the cell, but something is urging me forward. He must be cold in there. He must be feeling awful, even though he won't let any emotion show. The only thing I feel from him is an icy indifference bordering on menace. He is a dangerous, dangerous creature. The anima inside of me *knows* that.

Perhaps he killed because he liked to?

Nerves prickling in my veins, I take the track pants out from under my arm and hold them out to show him.

"Lia?" Savage's voice sails over to me. The rest of the dungeon is quiet.

"Just a minute," I say, keeping my eyes on the cold shark before me.

His eyes flick down to the pants, and *ever* so slightly, he cocks his head.

I take this minuscule movement as a sign I'm doing the right thing, so I levitate the bubble shield with the pants inside of it just in front of me.

The shark shifts in his chair.

Of course, being more than feral, Savage has preternatural instincts and notices something is up straight away, sticking his head as far as he can out of his own cell bars. "What's that?" he asks, and I can hear the amusement in his voice.

I levitate my little sphere through the bars of Scythe's cell and then I realise that I've not thought this through.

Scythe's eyes move from the pants to me as they levitate awkwardly in front of him. Clearing my throat, I steel myself and use a skill I don't often have to resort to.

It takes a fair bit of concentration, but I manage to make another shield in the shape of my hand and use that to manipulate the material. Lowering them to the ground, my phantom hands hold them out by the elastic waistband by his feet.

I glance back up at him, holding my breath. But

then he lifts his feet. I almost sigh in relief as I hoist the pants onto his feet and pull them up his calves and knees, noting the intricate tattoos there. I swear when I reach his thighs, though, not knowing how we're going to do this.

But the chains around his arms must not be super tight because Scythe lifts himself off the chair, and quickly, I pull the pants up and over his lap. I let go before I touch his skin... or dick with my phantom hands.

With the track pants on, he looks back up at me with absolutely no change in his face. I suppose he likes them if he let me put them on?

Trying not to think about it, and satisfied by this small success, I turn away and go to sit down in my usual spot between Savage and Scythe's cells.

I look at my steel door, releasing a breath as I turn towards Savage.

"What did you give my brother?" the wolf asks quietly, his handsome face serious.

Clearing my throat, I say softly, "A bit chilly in here, isn't it? I got him track pants."

A look I cannot interpret shoots across his face, but in a flash, it's gone.

Savage says in a voice quite unlike his usual flirty one, "A little bit less now though, princess."

I say nothing and close my eyes, suddenly struggling to concentrate on my patient.

Savage's voice regains its flirty attitude, and he says, "I think princess likes us, boys." I know he's grinning from ear to ear, and though it takes everything in me not to open my eyes and look at him, I can't help the smile that creeps across my own lips. The anima in me is a wanton thing because a wild heat sweeps through my insides at the pleasure I hear in his voice.

I clamp that shit down for all I'm worth because there is no way I can let it show.

Chapter 11

Aurelia

When the hour is done, I'm happy with the amount of progress I've made with my patient. I had to lower one of my inner, heavier shields at the end to get a boost of energy to push through, but it was worth it. With Savage and Scythe on either side of me, I don't feel like I'm in danger in this dungeon right now. I open my eyes and crack my neck with a groan.

I turn to find Savage watching me, his eyes half lidded. He seems to snap out of some reverie because his face comes alive. He gives me a slow, hot smile, and I can't help but notice how pretty his lips are.

He turns his head to scratch the right side of his neck with a dirty, bloodied hand and I still in shock as tsunami like force hits me in the gut. Everything in my universe narrows down to that single piece of Savage's skin.

Because sitting there is a golden, glowing symbol. A skull with five beams of light shooting out from it.

My mating symbol.

Savage pulls out a red foil lump from his pocket and I realise he's saved half the Hershey's Kiss from yesterday. He puts the rest of it in his mouth and savours it as I stare at him.

"What's wrong?" he asks around the chocolate.

It takes a monumental effort to move my head from side to side to shake it. "Nothing."

A cold, dark feeling consumes my heart, and something tells me to look at the cell behind me. Slowly, in a dazed trance, I get to my feet and turn to look at the dragon chained in his cell.

In the darkness, there is a golden glow, and it's on Xander's neck. My symbol is obvious through the gloom.

I don't breathe. I don't blink. I don't think.

Shit. Shit. Shit. Fuck. No. How?

My feet move of their own accord, something *more* than me guiding me towards Scythe's cell. He's sitting there as he always does, only this time It's not only his ice eyes that glow. It's the golden mark on the right side of his neck, beckoning to the deepest parts of my being.

My anima lets out a roar of sheer, joyous release, and my knees buckle. I catch myself with my shield just in time and make myself go still.

With the pressure of containing my emotions, an involuntary tear trickles down my cheek and Scythe's alert eyes follow its trail.

It's a blow to the gut. My insides are going to explode.

I have to get out of here. I need to leave and never come back. How could I have been so stupid? How could I not have known?

But I know exactly why. I've had seven shields around me, and I'd dissipated on of my psychic ones in order to get a better grasp on my patient today. I'd never let that shield down in front of the prisoners before and it was the one responsible for protecting me from external psychic forces—so it had also hidden their mating marks from me.

I want to be sick.

All three of these animalia are my mates. Three of the five I was promised to by fate.

I swallow through a sandpaper throat, knowing both Savage and Scythe are instinctually tracing my movements, pupils dilated. They do it because they are my mates and even if they can't see it, their animus is making them more responsive to me. To want to care for me. To want to kill for me.

Their beastly spirits know who I am. I can see that plain as day.

But their minds don't.

I turn on my heel and all but run for the exit, but it feels like I'm striding through water, my limbs slow and wobbly.

Savage's rough voice chases after me in a playful bound. "See you tomorrow, princess."

Thankfully, my time is up anyway, and Beak is smiling at me from the other side when he opens the door. The smile I give him is of genuine relief, and his face brightens with pleasure to see it. But my body does not respond to him in that desirous way it normally does.

Now that I've seen my mates, my body will never elicit that same response for anyone else.

I'm not prepared for the level of emotions I'm experiencing.

For animalia, the mating bond is the strongest

magic in existence and it is not in our nature to ignore it.

I stumble out of Halfeather's mansion in a dream-like haze. The world outside hits my retinas in a dazzling display of colour.

It's as if I'm seeing everything for the first time. My world had been black and white this morning. Now, I was seeing it in 4k with surround sound. My soul has woken up and is crying out in a happy song. *We've found our bonds,* she sings, *we're finally home.*

Beak says something to me as I fall into my car, but I don't hear him.

I don't even know how I get home, but I'm drenched in sweat when I do. Functioning on auto-pilot, I somehow get ready for work, the faces of my three mates flashing in my mind like a slideshow on repeat. My stomach is swirling, my brain is tumbling. I feel like I've been lost at sea and now the port is within view on the horizon, but I cannot set anchor. It's relief and pain. Happiness and despair.

My mind rages for the rest of the day, so much so that Aunt Charlotte asks me what's wrong multiple times. The third time I drop a can of tomato paste, she sends me outside for a time-out like I'm one of her naughty kids.

All I do when I go out to the loading dock is pace back and forth from the dumpster to the door. My mates are here. Does my father know? He can't know. Only the central mate, me, their regina, and the other males in the mating group can see the marking. They would've seen mine if I hadn't spent my entire life with a shield of magical titanium around my entire person. I'd had it drilled into me from the moment I'd returned from the oracle and she'd declared my mating group numbering five of the most dangerous animalia of our time. We should have known, being what I am.

With what I can do.

The anima in me wants me to get in my car and go back to them. It's demanding we go in there and jail-break my mates immediately. The desperate anima wants to mate with them and complete the bonding ritual—complete our union and make them mine. To join our power in a pool and share magic so intimately we all orgasm over it.

Fuck. Fuck. Fuck.

I can't do any of that. I'm sweating. I'm wet and aroused and wired to the extreme.

It's torture and I have no idea what to do. I pour water from my drink bottle into my cupped hand and splash it on my face. I slap my cheeks. I do star jumps to try and get rid of this insane energy I now have. Aunt Charlotte comes out to check on me, narrowing her eyes at my state. Then her eyes widen.

"What's happened?"

I scramble to save face. She can't know about this. No one can. If word gets back to my father, he'll have the three of them executed immediately.

In any other animalia, this would be cause for grand celebration. Finding your mating mark on another was a success story, something to brag about. Something you tell your girlfriends and the women in your family, and you all jump up and down and scream in happiness together. Your aunts would tell you how to deal with protective alpha mates and cry, telling you how happy they are.

There were parties, engagements, drinks and dresses. A normal girl would hug and giggle with her aunt.

But I'm not a normal animalia and I can't have them. I want to tear my hair out. I want to scream. Instead, I shake my head and grit out, "Too much coffee. Sorry."

She doesn't believe me, frowning and slamming the door shut behind her. She probably thinks I'm on drugs or something. In a way, I am.

I make it through the rest of the day, and eventually, I lie in bed that night. Sweating. Thinking. It is *madness* the level of lust I now have, pouring through me like bubbling champagne. There is no way I'm going to sleep this wet, this writhing for my mates. My mind is a haze of desire and all it does is think about those muscular bodies sitting there in that prison when they should be here with me.

Savage and those lips. Dear god, it's fodder for the biggest orgasm in the world. All this healing work has left me far more empty than any amount of burgers and thick shakes can refill, and an earth-shattering orgasm will fix me right up.

My mind is now fixed upon Savage standing behind the bars of his cell, with his low-slung jeans, covered in dirt, the sheen of his sweat highlighting the ridges of his muscled torso. My hands find my neck and trail their way down my body, caressing the mounds of my breasts. I imagine Savage's large hands stroking me down the swoop of my stomach and down the sheer fabric of my nightie. I hitch the hem up, dragging my fingers up the tops of my thighs and skimming my underwear.

I hiss, my back arching as I imagine Savage on top of me, his wolfish grin and hungry eyes waiting in anticipation. My right hand creeps into my panties while my left hand massages my breast. I circle my wet and throbbing clit, gasping at the feel of my own slick. I'm incredibly soaked and can't help but plunge my fingers inside myself, exploring my wet heat. Gods, what would it be like if he were really here? If any of my mating group were here, touching me, telling me I looked like a princess? I would simply die, I think; combust into a thousand flames of pleasure. My lips whisper their names into the dark of my bedroom. The names of my strong, dangerous mates emerge from my lips like prayer: *Savage, Xander, Scythe.*

Chapter 12

Savage

Here I am, lying on my comfy dungeon floor, when the melody of a song runs down my spine in a warm caress.

I sit bolt upright.

Xander and Scythe shift too, except no chains are clanking with their movements. My heart pounds as every part of my being stands to attention.

I look over at Xander and realise that while his physical body is still chained to the wall, his astral body has woken up, blue-grey, transparent and frowning down at himself. I look down at my own body and see that I'm also blue-grey and see-through. My body still lies on the stone floor, eyes closed and asleep.

I barely have time to admire my own face before

my attention is pulled by another, heady, quivering note.

Magic as old as time itself is in the air; delicious, strong, lusty.

Something has bypassed the magical shield around the dungeon and it can only be one thing:

The call of our regina. Our central mate.

I close my eyes and allow the song to take me, knowing the others will follow their instincts and do the same. It's too enticing to deny, and the animus in me roars with happiness.

Our mate is calling for us, and by all the fucking wild and beastly gods, I want to scream to her that I'm coming.

I float upwards on the melody, my cock twitching and excitement spinning through me. I get to see my regina. I get to see the woman I'm destined to spend the rest of my life with, to worship, to fuck, to make love to, to... fuck.

Passing through the levels of Halfeather''s mansion, the night sky meets me with a thousand twinkling lights. I grin like a madman to be in the outside world again after so many months. I can't see my bond-brothers, but I know they'll be carried in by the melody of her song too.

I'm pulled through the night, over the highway

and through suburbia and I memorise the way there —it's imperative that I find her after we find a way to escape our imprisonment. The current lowers me towards a tiny, dilapidated unit, no more than a bungalow, set deep up a long drive behind another larger house. Adrenaline pounds through my body as the magic deposits me outside a bedroom window. I pass easily through the glass and into a small, darkened room where I feel Scythe, Xander, and two other shadowed presences with us—the fourth and fifth members of our mating group to complete our merry band of nutcases. I've never met them face to face, but I know they've been pulled here to satisfy our regina, same as me.

Speaking of our woman, she is, at present, writhing around on her bed in a tiny, thin, pink nightie, one hand in her panties, her eyes closed. Holy fucking Mother of all...

It's Lia.

Her black hair is spilling around her head, loose from her ponytail, her beautiful face a mask of pleasure, pillowy lips parted. Long, shapely legs squirm on the bed and I'm struck by the desire to jump on top of her. I can't believe fate brought her to us in our jail.

The mating mark on her neck glows in the night,

as if it's happy to see us and the sight of it has me choked up. I've been looking for that mark my entire life. How the fuck didn't I see it before now? And her scent... by the gods, it's like a drug for me and all I can do is close my eyes and savour it.

I knew she'd smell delicious. Like cupcakes and vanilla and strawberries. I really do want to devour her whole.

She must sense us because her eyes fly open and she blinks up with those blue eyes I want to drown in.

Her hand stays between her legs as she whispers in confusion. "What the..."

I look around and see the other males are motionless, probably dealing with their hard-ons or shock or whatever. But I'm ready for action, as always. I practically leap forward, half wanting to replace my hand with hers, half wanting to show her I'm not a pervert. But her scent is too strong for me to resist. With my heart pounding like a mad drum, I lean over her and whisper, "Lia? You've let out a siren call to your mates. That's why we're all here."

Chapter 13

Aurelia

In my dream, my room is full of shadows, but I'm not scared at all. If anything, these dark figures are a comfort.

I'm so horny I could burst. It's come over me hard and strong, a sweeping desire tumbling through me like a tsunami, waves of lust making me want to spread my legs as wide as they will go.

And then one of the shadows steps forward and I recognise his wolfish face straight away. Savage. Looking down at me with such burning desire. I thank my lucky stars that my subconscious has given me exactly what I need right now. The mating mark on his neck glows bright and sharp. Eagerly, I reach for him.

"Come here, Savage," I say longingly, without

any shame at all because that's the one benefit of this not being real. He hesitates and my voice takes on a sensual whisper. "Please?"

Thank all the gods he doesn't need any more encouragement, because he falls into my arms and captures my lips with his. His skin is hot through my nightie and I arch into his hard muscles. He groans, sweeping his tongue into my mouth, devouring me as if he's been waiting an entire lifetime to do this. He tastes me and I allow him access to everything he wants, curling my legs around him. He breaks our kiss, leaving my head spinning as he runs his tongue down my neck and over my mating mark.

This is perfect. So bloody perfect, and exactly what I need.

"Oh gods," I moan, and my voice makes his movements frantic. "I need you inside me."

"Lia," he groans against my neck as if my voice pains him but his hand finds my breast and squeezes gently.

What a fucking wonderful dream, but I'll have to thank myself later as I hiss again. Savage pulls down the top of my nightie to lick my nipple, sweeping his hand down the length of my body, leaving flames where his skin touches mine. He hooks his fingers into my panties and pulls them gently down.

Drawing away from me, he quickly drags my underwear down my legs, and then he's back on top of me, grinding an impossibly hard erection into my centre with his jeans still on.

I'm so fucking happy about this. I might not be able to have my mates in real life—but in dreamland? It's the next best thing.

I make a sound of dissatisfaction. This isn't fast enough. My anima wants him naked between my legs. I need all of him, all of *them* like my life depends on it.

The other shadows around us seem to darken, and I glance at our onlookers. I can just make out four broad shapes but no details—as if they don't want to step forward and be known just yet. I find that I don't mind being watched, though. If anything, it gives a kick to my desire. Let them see. Let them all see what their regina looks like when she needs them.

They are my mates and I *want* them to be here and see me naked and in pleasure.

"Eyes on me, princess," Savage growls jealously. The raw hunger in his eyes is enough to set me tingling and I'm mesmerised by his desire for me. This pure, hungry predator who wants to devour me whole. He says darkly, "I want to be inside you while you squirm."

I gasp as he slips his hand between my legs and groans deep in his throat. He closes his eyes in pleasure, fingers exploring my wet core. I wriggle around him and he chuckles before plunging a finger inside of me.

I let out a strangled moan, arching my back and spreading my legs wider for him, a silent command to go deeper. I reach for his arm, enjoying the feel of his thick muscles flexing. He grins down at me, and then presses his lips against mine. I kiss him excitedly, holding his face, feeling his rough scruff under my fingers.

My anima keens for more and I must say it out loud because he whispers against my lips, "Greedy princess, wanting more. You want me to fill you up, don't you? You want all of us fucking you until you can't scream anymore, don't you?" His fingers plunge in and out of me to the beat of his words, and I can only writhe as tendrils of warm, dizzying pleasure ripple through me like the most delicious summer wind.

"Yes, Savage," I moan. "I want it all."

"Say please."

My eyes fly open and I find his eyes dark and

serious. He reaches up and pulls my hair tie from my hair, already loose from my writhing, and puts it on his own wrist. "So beautiful," he breathes. "*Now say please.*"

I bite my lip as he makes slow strokes inside of me, his thumb brushing delicious circles over my clit. How I want this to be real. How much I want to please him. So I say it with lusty relish, "Please, Savage."

He plunges a second finger into me, and I whimper at the stretch. He increases his speed, the wet sounds of my own pussy winding me tighter and tighter, pushing me over the edge. I burst into a thousand pieces, screaming out his name as he buries his face in my neck and groans. I gush all over his fingers and he wrings every last moment of pleasure from me. He pulls away and I look up at him with a half-lidded gaze, his hazel eyes hungry, his beautiful lips parted. Even in my dreams, my mate made sure I got what I needed. It makes my anima flutter with happiness.

I sigh in satisfied pleasure, but then Savage is suddenly off me, standing next to my bed. Without taking his eyes off mine, he raises his fingers and puts them straight into his mouth, closing his eyes as if savouring the taste. I stare at his mouth in awe.

He frowns when he pulls his fingers out. "Fuck, princess. I can taste you even in this form."

But my eyes are fluttering shut, my body like butter, melting into my bed in the wake of the most mind-shattering orgasm I've ever had. I allow myself to be boneless, a contented smile tugging at my lips. When was the last time I'd felt this... happy?

Dear gods, if only all dreams could feel this real.

Chapter 14

Aurelia

The next morning, I wake up with the most heavenly afterglow still clinging to me like golden morning dew. I smile as I stretch out luxuriously on my bed and find the mess I'd made of my sheets. My underwear is on the floor and I chuckle as I bend to pick it up.

That was a bloody great dream and I'm *so* keen to do it all over again tonight. If I have that experience to come home to every day, perhaps... just perhaps, it will be enough to get me through the rest of my life without my mates.

I haven't slept so well in ages and my little fantasy even has me humming as I strip my bed of my sheets and shove them joyfully into my thousand-year-old washing machine. From my old laptop, I put some music on, bopping my head as I shower and get ready to head back to Halfeather's mansion.

The buzz I have is more than a post orgasm after-glow; my skin is practically luminescent with my power coursing through me in strong waves. I could very well get heaps of progress with my prisoner-patient today and be done with Halfeather's lecherous gaze sooner than planned. I flex my fingers and feel my power thrumming through me. Hell, I might even be done today.

As a dark pang shakes my heart, I tell myself that this will be good. Because then I can leave those males behind and move on with my life. The more time I spend with them, the harder the separation is going to be. My anima is writhing rebelliously within me today, hissing and flapping with excitement to see them again. I muzzle that sensation as quickly as possible.

So it's with great determination that I rock up to Halfeather's mansion with Maisy sparkly clean after a quick wash this morning.

"You're in a good mood," Beak says as he opens my door. Then he drops his voice in what I think is jealousy. "Some beast treating you well?"

"Why does it have to be some guy, huh?" I say, playfully poking him in his oversized bicep. Yeah, at least I got to touch *someone* before I left this place. "Maybe it's all just me."

He grins and I smirk at the way his tawny eyes gleam, checking me out. If I can't have my mates, I could in theory, choose a human to spend my life with. A beast would figure out what I am as soon as I had intimate contact with them and that information would then be valuable and *very* sell-able. No, humans are my safest bet.

But as soon as that thought enters my mind, my stomach churns and I have to press my fingers over my mouth to stop the urge to vomit. I sigh at my anima growling angrily at the prospect of being with a beast other than one of my mates. I sour immediately as I follow Beak inside. Unexpectedly, he turns around to glance at me, his eyes swooping down my body.

All of a sudden, I'm cognisant of how I've dressed myself while my mind was busy re-living my dream this morning.

I'm in a *dress*. One of two that I own. It's maroon, tight, plunges a little low, and I remember putting lipstick on. I had been buzzing with power and lust and I'd had no fucking idea that I was preening myself like a bird in heat. I'm in way over my head and I realise I've not even packed a jacket. My anima is aware that my mates are down there and everything inside of me has been waiting and ready to see their faces again. It's a *blatant* attempt for male attention considering how I've been dressing the other days. It's practically a giant, sexy, green flag that announces, "Woohoo, female ready and available!"

I'm *not* available! I'm the least available anima in the universe right now.

A panic attack is building up in me by the time we get down to the dungeon. I don't know how I'm going to hide this from Savage. He's going to know something is different right away. He's too observant of me. Too interested in me.

As a mate should be.

I'm fighting embarrassed tears as Beak opens the last steel door for me and gives me a hot look that turns into confusion.

I force a smile on my face and the movement calms me a little. If I'm going to keep these males safe from my father, I need to keep up appearances. *That* is the most important thing right now, emotions be damned.

So I plaster on an even wider smile on my face and all but strut past Beak and Scuff down into the dungeon corridor as if it's my personal runway. My step falters, but I pretend I'm an actress on set, putting on the show of a lifetime. *No one can know. No one can know. I'm just a regular, horny animalia. No mates here.*

But the deeper I get into the gloom of cold stone, I can *feel* that something is different.

It's deathly quiet today. And something heavy vibrates between the cells. A whisper of something powerful.

I avoid looking at Scythe and stride right past his cell, though I can see the gleam of his eyes on me. Savage is standing by his bars as usual, and as I walk up to my patient's steel door, my shields are back up at full capacity so I can't see his mating mark.

"Morning," I say briskly. But I stand there for a moment, trying to figure out what's changed in my wolf.

Savage has a grin that could light up the whole world at midnight, and it takes my breath away.

His hazel eyes gleam as he says in a low voice, "Hello, princess." Both of his large, tattooed hands grip the bars so tightly it looks like he wants to rip them apart. My eyes are drawn to something new on his left wrist.

He's wearing a black hair tie.

Time stops.

Horror winds its cruel way up my chest into my throat.

I breathe, "*No*."

Male arrogance drips off him like oil. "I had a fun time last night, princess. We all did."

My hand flies to my chest as abject terror spins through me. "Oh gods, I can't breathe."

Xander scoffs behind me as Savage gives a deranged cackle. "Yeah, I know, I know."

I glare at him. "W-What the hell is going on?"

"I believe," Savage says with vicious mirth, "I astrally finger fucked your sweet pussy and you came all over my hand."

My knees go weak and I have to crouch down to make sure the floor is under me. This is a bad dream. This has to be a nightmare. None of this can be real. This can't be happening to me. No one could be this unlucky.

I can't look at him and his arrogant, beautiful face, so I cradle my head in my hands and squeeze my eyes shut. I can still feel his fingers in me as I think about my own body. My pussy does feel like it's been stretched by fingers bigger than my own.

It *had* been real. I'd actually called them all in with a mating siren song. Do they know I'm their mate, then?

I take a deep breath and look up to see Savage watching me obsessively as he normally does, just with an arrogant, very-happy-with-himself smirk.

"I think I'm gonna be sick."

"Weak stomach, hatchling?" drawls Xander. "Might want to check you didn't catch a canine virus or something."

My stomach is churning now, but not in disgust, in sheer, unadulterated embarrassment. They'd all been there—even glowering Scythe—and had seen me naked and lusty, spreading my legs for—

Dear Wild Mother, get a grip, Lia. You're a woman, they're your mates. You have nothing to be ashamed about. Nothing at all because it's normal and natural. They're the ones who should be embarrassed.

I collect my blabbering mind together with this thought and promptly stand up, crossing my arms and level both Savage and Xander a glare. "I hope you enjoyed the show"—I raise my voice to make sure Scythe can hear— "even if the others were too cowardly to come forward."

They'd all been there. Five shadows. Shit. Now they all knew what I looked like.

Xander is still hidden in the dark of his cell, still,

as if he's imagining me from last night. I stand there and let him look at me in my dress, bare legs and all.

He flexes his wrists, and the chains around them rattle. "You're an arrogant little thing, aren't you? What's your anima and why can't we scent it?"

Panic makes my mind work at a thousand miles an hour.

"I don't answer to you, dragon," I shoot back, aggressively.

But then Scythe speaks from his cell behind me —a rasping voice that sounds like someone has sliced open his throat from the inside and let it scar over. "Why can't we see your mating mark today? What are you hiding?"

His voice, and the dark meaning behind his words is terrifying enough to give me goosebumps. But shit. They must've seen my mark last night.

I scoff to hide my rising terror and call back, "You're the ones in a dungeon, and you're asking *me* what I'm hiding? A bit rich, isn't it?"

This is bad. The three of them know. If they ever get out of here, they'll come for me. They won't be able to deny their own primitive instinct. My anima is calling out to their three animus' in a shrill mating call and I stomp on that immediately.

"I don't like you," says Xander.

Well, that is a good thing. I snap, "Yeah? Well, you're an asshole Xander, because I..."

I snap my mouth shut.

Savage remained quietly attentive while I snapped at the other two, but he presses me now. "Because what?"

Because there is something in my dress pocket that I made this morning when I'd been happy and clearly insane—I'd brought Xander a USB with new music on it, alright? But I can't very well say that out loud, can I? I inhale a calming breath, trying to ease my frazzled nerves. Then I create a shield-ball around the USB in my pocket, levitate it, invisible, through the cell bars and smack Xander on the head with it.

He flinches, but before it falls to the floor, I sweep it upwards and plug it into the device on his hip.

"Bunch of assholes, the lot of you," I scowl. "Now be good boys and stay quiet so I can concentrate on my patient."

My heart is pounding as I sit down on the floor and all I know is that I have to get out of here and never come back. For some reason, the three beasts *do* remain quiet, but I hear Savage sit down and can practically feel him poking my side with his stare.

Whether it's my anger at the three of them, or the actual power boost from one of my mates giving me an orgasm last night, I finish healing my patient within the hour. I prise the jaws of the shadow snake's teeth one by one from around the nape of his neck.

The entire thing dissolves in a mist of black magic.

Chapter 15

Aurelia

The satisfaction at perhaps the best healing job I've ever done barely registers, because as I get to my feet, I know I won't be back tomorrow. I know this is the last time I will ever lay eyes on my mates. I shouldn't do it, but the wild, primitive anima part of me steps between Xander and Savage's cells to take one last look at them both.

Xander's mouth scowls at me and I wish, just for a moment, that I could see his face properly. But he'll just have to stay as a shadow in my imagination.

Savage's hazel gaze is searching as he stands half a foot away from me, and I can almost feel the heat of his animus. If my shields were down, I would have been able to scent him, too.

Alas, I will never know what he really smells like. That is the worst thing of all. But it is a safety thing, and it's smart for me to keep it that way.

I could, in theory, *touch* him. He must think this too because he pushes one large hand between the bars, palm up like a peace offering.

I stare at it for a long, long time, and he stares back at me in silence. Something inside of me breaks a little as I close my eyes and turn away from him. My anima whines in sorrow.

"Lia." Savage's voice is surprised, like he doesn't understand what's going on. I want to say that I'm sorry. That I wish things were different. That if I were a different beast, I would be running into his arms right now, kissing him, rescuing him from his prison, taking him home with me.

But for both his and my safety, I can't reveal anything. I'm passing Scythe's cell before I know it and against my will, my head turns to look at him.

He glares at me as I force my feet to keep moving, and it's the coldest thing I've ever seen. I can't read his expression because there's literally nothing there. His face has been hewn from ice and all I can feel from him is that he hates me.

I didn't know my soul could feel so much pain until this moment.

When Beak opens the door for me, it's like I've surfaced from deep water. The heaviness around me suddenly dissipates, and I take a fresh breath.

"Are you alright?" Beak says, briefly putting his hand on the small of my back. I look up at him and smile at his kindness. I'll miss *that* too.

"I'm just happy because I'm done with the patient," I say. "I don't have to go down to that awful place ever again."

He nods as if he understands, but he doesn't smile back as I expected. "That's really great," he murmurs quietly.

Maybe he likes me after all and is thinking about how he'll miss me, too.

Back in Halfeather's office, the old eagle is dragging his eyes up my bare legs and I'm very grateful this is the last time I ever have to see him.

"I've done what I can for him, Mr. Halfeather," I say quickly. "It's up to him and his power to have him wake up now."

"Indeed?" he says slowly, eyes stuck like glue on me. "Well, I must say it pleases me greatly that this is not the last time we will be seeing one another."

My brows shoot up as I register what he is insinuating.

"Mr. Halfeather," I say, as if this is all a pleasant

joke. "I'm the consummate professional. I take it my father's debt is paid as we discussed?"

The corners of his mouth turn down. "Ah, that's the thing, Aurelia. Your father did not just sell me your services, my dear."

A chill consumes me as I suddenly realise there have been no signs that Mr. Halfeather has a mate. That is unusual for a wealthy male such as him—usually they are a rex for a group of mates, bonded by fate or not.

My voice drops an octave as a deadly stillness falls over me. "What were the terms exactly, Mr. Halfeather?"

A smile creeps over his mouth and he skulks towards me, his black robe swishing limply. "A bride contract. A princess of the Serpent Court. A worthy union, do you not think?"

I become stone. This whole thing is made worse by what had happened last night and the fact that three parts of my soul sit in a cell below me, so close that my body can still feel them.

A distant whistling sounds outside and I frown, because who the hell is whistling in this place? Halfeather is not the type of employer who would allow that. But no one responds to it.

It's then that the blue-grey astral form of Savage

strolls into the room with his hands in his pockets, whistling that happy tune, closely followed by a see-through Scythe, wearing nothing but track pants and a murderous expression, and a transparent Xander looking around with the strangest eyes I've ever seen.

I stare in horror at the three of them, this being the first time I can see Scythe and Xander properly.

Even in their ghostly astral forms, I can tell that all of them are apex predators of the highest orders.

They're all tall, and the three of them dwarf the room. Scythe, with silvery hair that brushes his shoulders, a wide, square jaw and high cheekbones. Marine animalia all share an impossible, cold, out-of-this-world beauty, and Scythe is no exception.

Xander's arrogant posture has him looking like he owns the place, and knowing he's a dragon, I guess that his own house is probably even bigger than this one. But one thing is clear and confusing to me: he's blind. Both eyes are silver all the way through, telling me that his physical eyes don't work. They glow with preternatural force, meaning he's seeing with his power. I can tell he's looking at me, and even sneering, his dragon's features are stunning. His torso is bare and there's tribal dragon markings in a full sleeve down his left arm. He has a black nose ring and a matching dangling cross earring on his left ear.

I'm aroused immediately.

The ghosts look around the room, then come to stand next to Halfeather, crowding around him as if they want to kill him. Savage sticks a hand through Halfeather's head and it goes right through. Halfeather, nor Beak or Scuff, show any sign of seeing them.

Savage gives a dramatic sigh. "Looks like we can't murder him right now, princess."

"Don't react to this," Xander sneers. "They'll think you're mad."

"I think I *am* mad," I blurt out.

Halfeather's brows shoot into his hairline as behind him Savage and Xander burst out laughing. But they're not nice laughs. Scythe simply glowers at me, probably taking offence, as most of his relatives probably *do* have the dreaded land-psychosis.

I swear inwardly, realising I need to ignore whatever is happening with these males in ghost form right now, because a very wealthy and powerful eagle is telling me something that is about to change the entire trajectory of my life.

It's also not lost on me that eagles and other birds of prey *eat* snakes.

I manage to unstick my lips and find my voice. "I *mean* to say, I'm afraid to disappoint you, Mr

Halfeather, but I am not a serpent princess. I have never pledged to my father's court, nor has he graced me with any titles. Nor am I, actually, a snake. I take after my mother, an Aquinas."

My surname is another lie. And the biggest one of all.

Savage and Xander suddenly stop laughing.

"And that is why this union is an excellent idea," says Halfeather, not perturbed by my speech. "We are both of the same order!"

Savage growls and I shoot him a look, but he only has eyes for Halfeather.

I stare at the old eagle, then glance around, more than aware of Beak and Scuff at the door, likely listening closely. Will they try and keep me here? Will they stop me if I try to leave? The thought of Beak tackling me down and dragging me back in here gives me the shivers and not in the sexy way. My three ghosts won't be able to do a thing to help me, either.

"I'm afraid there's been a mistake, Mr Halfeather, I—" I am very aware that if I deny this powerful man, there will be consequences. I need to make nice as much as it irks me. "I... must talk to my father about the particulars."

"You're kidding!" Savage exclaims. "You can't marry this cunt!"

"Of course, of course," Halfeather says smoothly, stepping back and bowing. "We must abide by the Old Laws, naturally."

"Motherfucker!" Savage exclaims, aiming a kick to Halfeather's legs, but of course, it sails right through.

I stiffen as Halfeather frowns down at his legs as if he feels the whisper of something. The Old Laws say that females are to marry as they are told to by senior males of the family, if they have no mates of their own. I plaster a smile on my face. "Indeed. I will get back to you, Mr. Halfeather."

"I would expect no less."

What an asshole. I turn on my heel and make for the door. Beak and Scuff hastily let me pass, their faces carefully blank, but I know that they are used to strange and unethical conversations in this office.

I all but storm back to the security desk, snatching my handbag when Beak holds it out. I stomp back to my car and gun the engine. I wonder why my three mates are suddenly able to move about in the mansion in their astral forms, and a dark feeling slides through me.

As soon as I'm past the boom gate and back on the road, I slap my steering wheel in anger.

Who the fuck does my father think he is, selling me like this? As the King of Serpents, he can do as he pleases with me and no one will question it. No one will care. I am actually powerless here. I was so close to going to college, so close to freedom! Angry tears trickle down my cheeks and I aggressively swipe them away.

I've been terribly naïve thinking my father wouldn't sell me at the first chance. I need to get as far away from here possible—far from my mates, from my father.

I'd fantasised about running away ever since he'd kicked me out. I'd planned the movements in my head, thought about the best places to go to hide from him. I'd just never had the gall to actually do it. But now? Now things are slipping out of my control so badly I'm thinking I have no other choice. If I want to take my life in my own—

"You're angry," comes a male voice.

I almost run my car off the road.

"Fucking genius, do you know that, Sav?" comes Xander's voice.

In my rear-view mirror are the astral forms of the

three males, sitting there like we're going on a school field trip.

"Fuck!" I choke out, indicating, then carefully navigating onto the gravel shoulder on the side of the road.

I pull up my handbrake and swing around to glare at them.

"Just what the hell do you think you're doing?" I cry.

Savage gives me a sheepish smile. "Sorry, princess, but I think you only have yourself to blame for this one. I think it's because of last night that—"

"What?" I exclaim. "You think just because you had your fingers in me you can just follow me around now?"

All three men glower at me.

"Well," says Savage, running a hand through his dark waves. "I *did* make you come."

"Just barely," I snap. "Get out of my car."

They all scowl in unison like they're triplets. Three, murderous, scary as all hell triplets.

"Leave!" I gesture to the doors.

"But this is too much fun, snake girl," Xander deadpans. "I'm not going anywhere until you tell us what you're hiding from your mates."

Oh, so I wasn't *'hatchling'* anymore. That stings more than it should. I turn back to face the front window and pinch the bridge of my nose, sighing deeply. Things couldn't get any worse. How am I supposed to run away with these three following me around?

My phone pings and I pull it out of my handbag to see a message from my father's assistant.

Chapter 16

Aurelia

DAD'S FUCKING LACKEY

What is your ring size?

How am I supposed to know? I don't even own any valuable jewellery, only the cheap kind I treat myself to each birthday.

Swearing under my breath, I glance back to see the three males sitting there and watching me as if they're deciding how they're going to kill me. If looks could kill, I'd be cinders already. Frozen cinders.

I think Savage is the only one who has any sort of positive feeling towards me right now. We are a right old happy family.

"Can't you guys go travelling somewhere else?" I

say irritably. "If you want to be out of your prison, then go wandering elsewhere."

Xander shakes his head, the single headphone wire he has in swinging. "We can't. Sav is connected to you because of last night, and he's pulling us along. We can't leave you in this form."

"Perfect," I mutter. "Just fucking perfect."

I sit there on the side of the road for a moment, simply seething and panicking and thinking. Everything is going wrong and I'm in way over my head. If I didn't know any better, my mates were the sort of males who were alphas—high-ranking members of their respective orders. I can't fathom how I'd ended up with them attached to me.

But it makes sense. So much sense that my anima is screaming that this is right and good and I need to do whatever they ask of me.

But I have more pressing matters to think about. I've been promised to Halfeather and there is no negotiating with my father about it. I look back at my phone.

DAD'S FUCKING LACKEY

What is your ring size?

I need to request a formal meeting ASAP. Emergency. PLEASE

I've never been allowed access to him directly, so I have to make appointments or beg his lackeys.

A black feeling is pouring through me, dark as smoke. I'm not going to get out of this. The only way is for me to leave.

"Are you actually going to marry that half-cracked egg?" Savage says in disbelief.

I don't look at them. I can't.

"Unless I run, I don't have a choice," I mutter.

They go quiet because we all know what a heinous crime it is to find your mates and not marry them. It's been done before, but it's looked down upon. The exceptions are made for rabid beasts and criminals of the worst sort.

Which three of my mates apparently are. They know this and so do I.

I have to ask them. "What did you do to get into Halfeather's prison?"

Savage lets out a huff. "You don't need to know that."

I clench my teeth and stare at my phone but there's no three dots suggesting a reply is coming. "Yes, I do."

"Why don't you look at us?" Savage asks angrily.

I bite my lip, but I'm also biting back tears and my stomach is a tumble of anxiety.

"Get out of the car, Lia," Scythe rasps.

The command in his tone angers me, even as goosebumps pucker my arms at the sound of his voice. Defensively I snap. "You can't tell me what to do."

Savage retorts, "Get out of the car and talk to us face to face. You're our regina."

This is the first time it's been said out loud and it hits me across the head like a baseball bat in a full swing. "I'm not," I say through gritted teeth.

"What?"

"You're mistaken."

Xander scoffs. "Snake's a liar now, too. Not surprised."

My heart aches as I say it. "You're not understanding," I say calmly. "Whatever you saw last night was just wishful thinking."

"Why are you doing this, Lia?" Savage asks. "Why don't you want to be our regina?"

Every time he says my name, something inside of me dies a little. But I have to convince them. Males like these won't give their regina up without a bloody battle. So, slowly, though it takes every ounce of discipline within me, I turn around to face them.

Even in their astral forms, their eyes burn holes into

me. They are so still, but the energy crackling between us is pulling me towards them. My anima goes wild within me, keening, trying to claw itself out of my skin.

"It's not that I don't *want* to be your regina," I say quietly, "but you must listen to my words right now. I am *not* your regina."

The expressions on their faces would make any animalia cower and I'm just grateful I don't have their actual forms sitting in my car.

"You can fucking feel it," Savage exclaims. "I know you can!"

I look at him and scream, "Look at my neck!" I jab my finger at my neck, where I know they can't see our mark. "Can you fucking see anything, Savage?"

He quietens then, staring at my neck, his face stormy with repressed rage. But his presence, Wild Goddess, his presence is a rumbling glimmer at the edge of all things.

Breathing hard, I repeat in a voice of deadly calm, looking my mate in the eye. "Can. You. See. A. Mating. Mark?" I swallow and look at Scythe and Xander in turn. "Because I sure can't."

I turn back around, blowing out a god forsaken breath. There's a curse on me, I just know it. How can someone get so much bad luck in such little time?

Someone shifts behind me and I freeze on instinct as Xander's molten voice whispers in my ear, so close I swear I feel his breath. "You're a liar, *snake*. And when I get out of this dungeon, I'm going to hunt you down."

My blood rages and my magic flares up. I slam the full extent of my psychic shields down, all but making me invisible. Their astral forms are forced from whatever is tying them to me and sent back into their bodies where they belong.

A presence like the old parts of the ocean sits heavy at the edge of my shield. I'm compelled by a force greater than me to turn around.

Scythe is still sitting there, looking at me. My heart leaps into my throat.

"What the hell..." I breathe.

He cocks his head, assessing me in a purely animal way, completely unbothered by my magical attempts to push him back. No one should be able to fight that. Literally no one except my father.

I don't think I'll ever get used to his damaged, raspy voice when he speaks. And with the full force of the ocean behind the promise in those ice-blue eyes, he says, "I'm going to find out your secret."

With that, he allows my magic to send him back.

My heart pounds in an unsteady rhythm, and it still does long after I get back on the road.

When I get back home, I'm surprised to see both Uncle Ben and Uncle Ron gardening in the back veggie patch. Ben isn't supposed to be back for another week.

Ben waves as he sees me drive in and it's like the pressure of everything that's just happened recedes. Grinning, I wave back. He's the only half decent person in my father's court. He's never hissed at me, never glared, never done anything other than treat me like a real person. Ron, on the other hand, looks at me warily and heads back inside the house with a plastic bowl full of freshly pulled carrots.

I race out of my car to go and see him. He's not a handsome guy, my Uncle Ben, but I've always found a real beauty in his rounded face and kind eyes. He's pale from his mining work, red-cheeked from weeding in the sun, and he sweeps off his straw hat as I reach him.

"Hi, Uncle Ben!" I say excitedly. "You're home early."

"Yes, love," he says, and I can't help but notice his smile is strained. "How are you?"

"Oh, just great," I lie. "Is everything alright with work?"

He grimaces and scratches the back of his neck. "It's going alright, up there. Busy, you know."

Behind him, Aunt Charlotte opens the kitchen window and Ben whirls around to see her glaring at us. She must've closed the shop early today, and I wonder if she knows about my father's plans. She'd never say anything to me though. The loyalty between the two siblings is like cement.

Ben's cheeks flush as he turns back around. All this worries me. Perhaps all isn't well at the mines. Whatever it is, though, I'm sure my father will fix him up with a better job.

"I'll bring you some dinner tonight," he says quietly. "Ron's making spaghetti meatballs."

"My favourite." I grin.

All dinners that aren't two-minute noodles are my favourite.

Chapter 17

Aurelia

I should have known Uncle Ben was trying to warn me with the meatball thing.

Not two hours later, I'm sending more messages to my father's assistant, demanding to speak with him, when Aunt Charlotte knocks on my perimeter shield. I let her in and skulk to the door.

She stands on my welcome mat with my four-year-old cousin, Trixie, who's jumping up and down with excitement, her blond curls swinging. I raise my brows at the black dress bag Charlotte's holding.

"What's this?" I say carefully.

Charlotte jerks her chin to tell me to allow her inside my house and I oblige, frowning at them both. She's dressed in a stylish red dress and her hair is freshly curled, as if she's going to an event. Her other five kids are at school. My father demanded the serpent population have as many children as possible to repopulate after the 70's purge.

"It's so exciting, Lia!" Trixie squeals. "I wish *I* was getting married!"

A dagger of white-hot horror pierces my core. "*What?*" I cry. At that moment, two snakes stroll up to the door, female scouts, both with unsheathed daggers angled at me. One of them runs her tongue over her bared teeth as she looks me up and down.

"We're to make sure you're dressed appropriately for Halfeather," she says through a smoker's throat. "Hurry up, you have twenty minutes."

Aunt Charlotte huffs and sweeps into my bedroom without another word. I wouldn't have followed, but Trixie grabs me with her little hand and hauls me after her mother, humming a wedding march under her breath.

Shit.

I mentally kick myself. I should have left immediately. I have a bag packed and everything in my closet—all the essentials, my entire stash of savings, passport, underwear, tampons, *everything*. This is happening too quickly. My father is a brilliant tactician. He'd probably guessed about my plans and known that me running was a possibility. The smartest thing for him to do is to secure this marriage straight away.

If only I'd been more clever.

Trixie unceremoniously shoves me into the bathroom, tapping her bare wrist as if she has a watch on it.

I shower, rapidly trying to think of an escape route out of here. I could easily turn into a rat or mouse or possum and get out of my window. But how long would I last out in the world without my phone and money and clothes? I am well and truly screwed.

Trixie opens the bathroom door and shouts excitedly at me and I hastily get out and towel off. When I arrive back in my room, there's a dress hanging from my curtain rail. I stop dead, looking at the long length of thin black silk.

It's a traditional serpent *wedding* dress. Slinky so that it will cling to my body and thin so that it leaves nothing to the imagination. In the Old Way, everything needed to be on show for the groom and his family to see exactly what they were getting.

Dear Wild Mother, I'm going to faint. I grip the edge of my door, sagging a little while Charlotte *tsks* and rummages through my drawers, completely invading my private spaces. I thought this was a formal engagement or something, but they'd only dress me up like this for an actual wedding.

"Hurry up!" comes a gruff shout from behind me.

I flinch violently and turn to glare at the two serpent females of my father's court smirking at me. Scowling, I step inside my room and slam the door in their faces. Their cackles come through the door, grating and wild; a herald of my doom.

"Hurry, Lia!" Trixie said. "Look, I'll even turn around, see?"

Charlotte slides the dress off its hanger and brings it over to me. She sniffs as if this is all very beneath her. "No underwear. That's how we all did it. That's the proper way."

"I need a bra though," I say, trying to get around her to my underwear drawer.

"No," she says sharply.

I stare at her, mouth agape. "My nipples will show right through that!"

She gave me a droll look as if to say, *that's the point.*

The Old Laws can get fucked, honestly. I don't even have any pasties or tape of any kind.

I snatch the dress from her and drop the towel,

ignoring her completely as her piercing brown eyes sweep comparingly down my naked body.

If only she knew that I'd had my five mates staring at my naked, writhing body just last night. Her eyes are *nothing*.

A pang of sadness cleaves at my heart at the thought of my mates.

The silk of the dress is beautiful, with tiny, barely there straps and a swooping back that comes down low. In any other situation, I would have *loved* this dress. It somehow hugs my curves in the most perfect way. It's the nicest thing I've worn in seven years and makes me look like a real woman.

It's as if it comes from a family who loves their daughter. Father is probably trying to create the illusion of it—of my value. Just for a moment, I stand in front of my mirror, look at myself, and can see someone else. Someone who is going to marry her mates in a dress given to her by loving parents. There'd be black and red roses on my side of the family and every colour of flowers under the sun for my mates. Wolves, sharks and dragons would be at my imagined wedding. There'd be an extraordinary variety of foods; raw fish for Scythe's family and a spit roast for the wolves. Wealthy and respected members of the community would be excited to see the serpent bride and her five grooms.

Trixie makes *oohing* sounds, running her hand down the long train, and it snaps me back to reality.

Aunt Charlotte makes a noise in the back of her throat, her red lips twisting as she looks at me. My cheeks are wet and I hastily wipe at them. "Halfeather will be happy and that's all that matters," she says quietly, almost to herself. "Now, what should we do with all this unruly hair of yours?"

Chapter 18

Aurelia

We arrive at Halfeather's mansion in the serpents' Mercedes, with my hair in a fancy up-do and Trixie in a poofy flower girl's dress complete with a slick ballerina bun. I hadn't been allowed to bring my phone, nor my wallet, or anything at all. Charlotte had merely put a diamond choker—a gift from Halfeather—on me, shoved flats on my feet—Halfeather is too short for heels to be a good look—and pushed me inside the waiting car where Uncle Ron and Uncle Ben avoided my gaze.

I get out carefully, my nipples fully peaked and visible in the chill breeze, and I have to suppress the urge to rub them flat. What a fucking mess. My heart pounds in my ears as Trixie takes my hand, batting her eyelashes at me, the *bride*. In a mild panic, I search the mansion as if I'll find friends here.

It's as if I'm seeing the place for the first time and the polished Grecian pillars are now the ugly bars to the cage of matrimony. This is to be my new residence. My new prison.

Beak and Scuff greet us at the door with grim faces. Beak won't look at me at all, and the tight leash I've been keeping on my fourth shield slips.

I might have done it on purpose, but I won't let myself think of why. Savage appears at my side, bursting with questions. Scythe and Xander stride out of the mansion a second later, trying not to be obvious about their eyes taking me in from head to toe—or more likely, head to nipples. I work hard to ignore them all and focus on following Beak and my uncles inside.

"That's a pretty dress, princess," Savage drawls, but his voice is tight. "You were pretty rude shutting us out— Oh fucking hell."

Savage notices my father waiting in the entrance hall.

The Serpent King stands, tall and menacing, an aura of dark power about his body, and barely looks at me. He kisses Charlotte on both cheeks and nods his satisfaction at her getting me here. Trixie skips up to him and he kisses her possessively on the head.

She is a princess of his court, of course she gets royal treatment. A spear of jealously hits me, and I'm immediately ashamed of being jealous of a child.

"Father," I say in what I hope is a cold, imperious voice. "We need to talk."

Savage and the males go quiet next to me and I can feel them there, almost flanking me like guards. But that was just my anima reaching—looking for people on my side when there aren't any.

"We do not need to talk, Aurelia," he replies coldly. His eyes flash in warning and a hint of shadow coils around his hand. "Your marriage to Halfeather happens now." He'll use his snake on me here, I know it. He won't care if anyone sees. Obedience is all that matters to him, and back-talk can get me in serious trouble.

I think about it for a moment, my eyes darting around to see if I have any exits.

"Not so strong now, snake girl?" Xander's snide voice comes in my ear and I want to cry. "You're going to be a plaything for this old eagle. I wonder if he'll let you out of your cage a few times a year?"

Biting the inside of my cheek before I completely lose it, I stalk forward. My arms are still crossed because I don't want Beak and every male beast in this room to see my nipples still taut from a chill that has nothing to do with the temperature of the room.

Silently, I follow the group, with Beak, Scuff, and my mates close behind me. My blood is pounding in my ears as we reach a new room, a sort of drawing room on the ground floor. We stop outside as my father strides in, followed by Charlotte, Uncle Ben, Uncle Ron, and Trixie, who skips through as if this is actually a wedding procession. My stomach churns, and I glance over my shoulder.

Savage, Xander and Scythe are silently glaring at me, as if they hate me for what is happening. As if it's my fault. But Beak is giving me a look of warning—an order to get moving. I scowl at him and he has enough shame to look away.

I turn around and walk through the door as Savage says, "Want me to kill him for you, princess? I didn't know you were a *real* princess."

"Your father doesn't like you very much, does he, little snake?" Xander drawls. "I wonder what bad thing you did to make him hate you."

Being born. That's the bad thing I did.

I swallow my pride as I walk into the drawing room where everyone is waiting for me in position around a lacquered wooden table.

Halfeather stands there, his receding scalp extra shiny as if someone has polished it for him, just for today. His eyes greedily take in my body. I dully wonder if that'll be one of my jobs as his wife, scalp polishing.

An older male I don't know—a tiger, I think—wears a formal suit and holds a folder full of papers. Likely a Council member to witness our union. Tigers are favoured for such things because they are usually impartial loners.

Halfeather rushes forward to take both my hands, eagerly kissing both, and I feel a hint of tongue. I shudder as he looks up at me with shining brown eyes.

"So beautiful, Aurelia. What a sight for an old *bone* like me."

I freeze in horror as I register the emphasis on that one particular word. An odd choice of wording made very purposefully in front of others.

He knows what I am.

My eyes slide to my father, who is smiling mildly, then Uncle Ron, who is staring at his feet. Holy Mother, they've told him, and that's why he's so ecstatic to marry me. This is no normal marriage.

Halfeather will get me pregnant immediately to produce more of me. He'll likely get others to do it too. The smartest thing to do would be to diversify the genes of my children to create the most powerful court since ancient times.

I wonder if I can turn into a mouse and scurry out the window, never to be seen again. But snakes eat mice. So do eagles, and my father is giving me a dark look that promises murder if I act out.

But I *could* turn into a tiger if I wanted.

Or a lion.

I've never tried it, but I could probably turn into a dragon, too.

I could destroy this house and everyone in it, if I wanted to. But then everyone would know that my mother was from the ancient house of Boneweaver. That we could turn into any beast we wanted as long as we'd been in physical contact with it.

But to do that would mean that everyone would find out and there would be a global manhunt for me. The valuable anima who could produce more of her kind. And a group of males and females who could turn into any beast? That court would be the most powerful group in known history. The Council wouldn't allow it, and every underground mob boss would be after me. Chain me up and use me to breed.

So as Halfeather leads me to the table in front of

the tiger councilman, I let him, holding back the burning of my eyes with all my might.

I glance over my shoulder again to see my astral prisoners watching everyone and everything closely. Scythe has disappeared and Savage stands by my elbow, peering over my shoulder to look at the papers. He lets out a breath that I swear I can feel and I shiver.

Halfeather brings out a tiny blue velvet box and my heart gives an unsteady beat.

"Perk up, little snake," comes Xander's voice on my other side now. "You're going to be living in a mansion instead of that old hovel of yours. You can come and visit us every day." And then closer to my ear. "He'll make you fat with little bird babies. How many do you want?"

I suppress a gag as Halfeather unceremoniously takes out the ring and grabs my hand. It's a huge diamond, round cut with a golden band. Halfeather gives me a haughty look as I stare at the massive rock, wondering how much I can trade it in for.

There has to be a way to get out of here, surely? Somehow, I can escape, I just know it. A piece of paper means nothing. Not to me, anyway.

"Sign here, please," the councilman slides forward a thick parchment and Halfeather picks up the pen and scribbles in an impatient but elegant cursive. Just as I go to take the pen, Halfeather hands it over to my father. My hand hangs lamely in mid-air for a single, disbelieving moment.

Xander chuckles softly behind me. "The snakes follow the Old Laws, eh? Nice little loophole for your filthy kind. They should have executed you all back in the old purge."

A chill creeps down my spine at the cold malice in my mate's words, but I have no time to ponder Xander's hate because I'm watching my father.

He signs the form in one brisk movement that tells me exactly what little importance I am to him.

And here I am, officially being given away as breeding stock.

Chapter 19

Aurelia

Charlotte, Trixie, and my two uncles leave the room, my heart pounding faster and faster with every step they all take away from me. I glanced at Halfeather, who's looking at me greedily. My cheeks heat up and my entire body prickles with adrenaline. How long will he wait to consummate the marriage? Because, honestly, he looks like he wants to do it right now.

I glance at Beak in alarm, and he shifts uncomfortably when he returns my look. There'll be no help for me here. He can't step out of line with his boss, that's for sure. I don't want to get him in trouble, either.

"She'll spend one last night at her own house," my father says, "as we agreed, Charles."

My heart leaps into my throat. Is it possible? I look between the two males and the remaining councilman, who nods. "As per the Old Laws."

I had forgotten about that particular rule. After marriage, the bride went back to spend one last night with her female family members while the males of her family stayed at her husband's home to make sure it was up to scratch. The next morning, the bride would then return to her new house. It was a thing from a time long past, when the bride needed to be instructed on how to bed a man properly. Such a thing could only be spoken about to a married woman, of course, so the separation was necessary.

The whole thing is stupid, but I'm not complaining. The fire leaves Halfeather's eyes, but the look he gives me before I leave is a nasty promise of what's to come.

I cringe as I stride out of the mansion to the solitary waiting car, crossing my arms over my nipples again and almost cutting myself on the giant diamond I'm supposed to now wear. I glance behind me to see if my astral prisoners are still here, but it's only Beak and Scuff who stand next to my father, Uncle Ron, and Uncle Ben. I shove my fourth shield up again, completely unwilling to let my mates back into my life. My heart keens for them to return to me, but two of them hate me and the third just wants to fuck me.

What a piece of rotten luck that I had been born the way that I had.

When I get back to my house, five snakes—female guards from my father's court—greet me with a collective menacing *hiss*. They'll be 'guarding' my house tonight, Charlotte tells me with a grimace, but I know she really means they're here to stop me from running.

* * *

It's midnight when I feel a familiar presence pounding on the outside of my shield.

"Aurelia? Aurelia!" Uncle Ben's panicked voice sounds from outside. I lower my house shield and he lurches towards my front door.

There's real terror in his voice. Something is deathly wrong. I rush to the front door and throw it open. "I'm here, Uncle Ben! What's happened?"

Outside, my serpent parole officers are nowhere to be seen.

Uncle Ben rushes to me, still in his tartan summer pyjamas, his eyes wild, arms reaching out for me. He roughly shakes me by the arms. "Aurelia, you need to leave, right *now*."

That sense of dread I feel is suddenly in my throat. "Why?"

"Halfeather's mansion has just been burnt to the ground. Everyone is dead. Halfeather, the staff, all murdered. Just one security guard escaped. Ron and your father are fine. I've sent the guards there to retrieve him as a ruse." My blood pools into my feet as a sinister cold sweeps over my entire form. If anyone from my mating group had died, I would have known about it. Felt it. But I'd not felt—

"Aurelia, the prisoners in Halfeather's dungeon have all escaped somehow. And Beak, the security guard, said one of them kept repeating a name over and over again."

I already know whose name would be on the lips of the prisoners.

Uncle Ben is frantic. "Aurelia, Beak said it was one of the Slaughter Brothers, the wolf, who kept saying your name. He told me to secure you. Your father is telling everyone you caused the fire to get out of the marriage."

Shock at the injustice of this hits me like a blow to the head. But I don't need Uncle Ben to tell me to leave a second time. While I run to my room, Uncle

Ben takes my keys and runs to get my car warmed up. I grab my duffle bag, shoving my wallet and the remainder of my hidden cash in it.

Once my father knows I've run, he will freeze my bank account or track my debit card, so I have to rely on cash from now on. I bolt out of my house, quickly checking the night sky for any sign of the sweep of a dragon's wings.

They know exactly where I live and having been pulled here once, they'll come to check here first... except they also know my car! I swear internally as I pull my house door shut and bolt to the driveway. I need to shield my car as well, then.

Uncle Ben gets out of the car and yanks his wallet out.

"Take this." He's holding a couple of notes.

He is already taking a great risk. "Uncle Ben, I—"

"Aurelia. Your father will have your head for running. You know that. You'll be on your own now. You need everything you can get. This is the best I can do for you."

The backs of my eyelids burn as I nod and accept the few notes he's holding out.

"Go, Lia. And fast."

Throwing my bag and then myself into my car, I

hit reverse and head out to the street, slapping a shield of invisibility over my car. This time of night, it will be fine to drive unseen, but once daytime comes and traffic increases, I'd be asking for someone to crash into me. Hopefully, I'll be far, far away by the time the sun clears the horizon.

Chapter 20

Xander

I stand with the Slaughter Brothers Inc. behind the smouldering ruin of Halfeather's mansion, wiping the old beak's blood off my face. Tearing Halfeather's skull in half had been both pleasurable and satisfying in every possible way. Burning his mansion to cinders with my own flames was another type of dream come true. I'd have to thank whoever had started the fire, but only dragon fire could turn a building like this to cinders.

We'd let the female staff go except one Scythe had tied up and thrown outside for the police with a message tied around her neck. Of the males, only Beak escaped, who Savage had really wanted to get his claws on for flirting with the snake girl. Before us stands her father, the Serpent King, looking down his nose at us with beady black eyes. Eyeing him with my magical sight, Mace Naga is shrouded in heavy, oily power. Scumbag serpent magic. The filthy, slithering creatures are known for it, and it's one of many reasons everyone hates snakes and the purge had been done, *and* why a dragon would never lower himself to deal with one.

The fact that my mate had come from this evil bastard? I've done many shameful things in my twenty-three years, but I've never been so ashamed in my life.

But as a member of this mating group, I am bound to help these males who have become my brothers. We are just as soul-bound to each other as we are to the snake girl.

We fight like brothers do, and it is just as well that these beasts are some of the few males who can handle my angry blows—Scythe had laughed the last time I'd landed a lucky blow and shattered his nose. The one and only time I *had* seen him laugh, crazy bastard.

So it was with great annoyance that our escape was stopped by a bunch of snake shitheads and their slippery king.

Savage had dragged me along to speak with the

father of the regina he was pussy-crazed for. Initially, I thought he'd wanted to kill the man, but something bigger is at play here.

"As loath as I am to admit it," the Serpent King says in a dull voice that has me instantly suspicious, "Aurelia organised this fire to kill us all. I believe her mates were in mind when she started it in the dungeons."

I narrow my gaze upon him, trying to detect any falsehood. But the truth is that I have been wondering why the fire started underground. The fact that he knows we are her mates is also surprising.

"She tried to kill us," Savage repeats, not quite believing his hot piece of ass would try and kill him. I've known all along she was capable of something like that, though. She *had* to be powerful to be regina to the Slaughter Brothers and me.

And she'd been lying to us the entire time she'd been down there.

Scythe is seething. I can see the icy cold force fluttering around him like lethal shards. He's livid about many things right now, but knowing that his regina is purposefully hiding herself is going to set him off on a rage, especially considering what had gone on between him and his own parents.

Hell, *I* was seconds away from shifting and launching myself into the sky.

Cracking my neck, I raise the volume on my device and change the song. It shuffles to one of the new songs the snake girl had given me. I rip the USB out of the player and throw it far into the grass.

Savage sees me, scowls, and runs to pick it up from the ground, cradling it to his chest as he returns to us. He sniffs it as if he can chase her scent on it. His nostrils flare as he tries to get a whiff of her and fails. He's been sniffing the foil chocolate wrapper every hour for the past two days, but hasn't been able to get a read from it.

"She's been hiding her scent from us." Savage frowns. He holds the USB up to Scythe, who takes it from him and sniffs it, too. I know already there's nothing to sniff on it, nor on the track pants she gave Scythe.

She's forgotten one thing, though. She let her protections down that night we were all at her house, and even in his astral form Savage was able to scent her properly when he tasted her.

Whatever her stupidity, these gifts had been cunning ways to manipulate us.

"Yes, that is a complication of her peculiar

powers," the Serpent King says. "That is why I need you, as her mates, to track her down. She needs to be stopped. She needs to be executed."

Fucking hell, he's outing his own daughter. The whole family is off. I thought mine were bad, but this guy is worse. At least my family keeps their punishments within the court.

"You want us to do it?" Scythe's rasp is raspier than ever from smoke inhalation, but there is no sign of pain as the Great White assesses the snake.

"She'll be charged for murder and sent to the prison for ferals. It will be a kindness to execute her."

Savage blows out a breath because he's been to that prison and knows what its like. I can see he's upset about his regina being taken away from him, the sappy bastard. But trying to kill us is a kind of blasphemy that beasts hardly ever see. It's a real sort of mad anima who tries to kill the other pieces of her soul group.

Fuck. I really do think she needs to die, and if she has no scent, Savage is the only one who can track her.

"We'll do it," I say, edging away from him.

Savage glances at me, then at Scythe. Our great leader doesn't make any movement, but that's normal for him. I glance his way and see a green aura of assent around his head.

"You must make a blood binding to the terms," the snake says. "Or she may try to manipulate you. You will recover her. You can do whatever needs to be done to bring her back, but you will *not* mate with her. When you bring her back, I'll deal with her the Old Way."

I roll my eyes at Savage, who is so pussy-crazed that he's foaming at the mouth to get back to her. I don't know if he'll agree, but this is personal now.

"Fine," Savage bites out. "We'll do it."

Shrugging, I offer my hand first to get it over and done with. The serpent brings out a ceremonial serpent dagger and pricks my index finger, muttering the binding over the wound. My entire finger burns like it's been stung by a bee.

The thought of mating with her makes me feel sick. She tried to manipulate us, then kill us, now she's run away from us all. It's not natural. It's a heinous crime, and though it's a shame I won't have a regina, I won't stand by such an insult.

"I agree not to mate with my regina," I say. "And I'll deliver her to you." Light flares from the cut and it becomes a coiled black marking.

If I mate with the girl, the thing will curdle my

blood and kill me from the inside out. When we return her, the binding will fade away.

Once he's repeated the ritual on the Slaughter Brothers, he says, "There. Now you are bound. Go and find my daughter."

Chapter 21

Aurelia

In my many fantasies about running away, I'd given a lot of thought as to exactly how I'd do it, and it is this that saves me now. I need to get as far away from Halfeather's mansion—and my father—as possible, and going north is my best bet. I imagine myself in a sleepy seaside town, going to the beach every day and working in the local coffee shop owned by a quaint family. In order to be completely safe from my father, I will need to move as many states away as possible, and going to the west coast is my best chance. I'll drive, keeping to the highway until I get as close to the border as I can manage, sleep during the day and travel at night when I can hide my car completely. It's a fool proof plan, because while my father can track my scent on foot, by car, it's a whole lot more difficult.

He'll never get the authorities involved. No, this ruse about me causing the fire is just to get the suspicion off him. I have no doubt that he'd married me to Halfeather and caused the fire that killed him. He's probably already received whatever sum of money he asked for and wants me back under his thumb.

The anima inside me wants to admit that my father's plan is brilliant.

But I'm not stupid either. I *can* do this. I will no longer cower in fear while men make decisions for me and force me to comply to their whims. I will not be prey. I will become the predator my mother's side of the family were. The ultimate predator of them all. I just need to gather my wits together and *do* it.

The excitement of making a new life for myself bubbles up alongside the adrenaline of running. Do I really think Savage and the other mates will hurt me if they find me? They are dangerous males, I have no doubt, and not at all that right in the head. I really have no idea what they will do if they catch me like they'd promised.

My best bet is to keep my secret safe and use it against them all.

I drive for four hours until the adrenaline fades

and turns into weariness. I stop by a petrol station to fill up, buy three energy drinks, and continue on for another hour and a half. As the morning traffic starts to pile up, I quickly check my phone for a nearby motel.

There's one owned by a lion family, and what a treat because snakes *hate* lions with a passion, so it will be an excellent cover for me.

I drive right to it with my eyes heavy and my limbs aching. It's a small but smart, clean-looking place with a gravel parking lot and single storey of suites. I could park, then shield my car and no one passing by would have any idea I was here. Very proud of myself, I park Maisy and head into the office where a young male lion, no more than a pimply teenager with a mop of blonde hair, smiles shyly at me. I pay him in cash and he hands me a shiny black key with a room number on it, as well as papers with a bunch of useless tourist information. I grin at him and go to find my room. I park my car a little way down from my room, so if my shield goes down due to tiredness, I still won't give my exact room away.

As soon as I get inside, I collapse onto the bed and fling up a light shield around the perimeter of the hotel so I'll be alerted if a snake enters the premises. Once I'm happy that I'm secure, I immediately fall into a deep sleep.

When I awake, dusk is settling around the motel and I feel a sharp pang on my shield. I sit bolt upright, my heart pounding as I register a serpent animalia entering the motel.

Not one serpent, *four*.

My father's lackeys are here. How the hell had they tracked me so quickly with no scent?

I close my eyes to hone in on my shield, but I can't do any remote viewing with my power—I can only feel who's inside. There are four of them, three men and a woman in their human forms. I recognise two of my father's retrieval squad, but not the other two. They head straight for reception, and I know right away they will threaten the young lion. As soon as they tell him they are here at the behest of the Serpent King, the cub will give me up for sure.

I need to get out of here.

Darting around the room, I collect my phone and duffel before throwing the key on the bed and rushing out the door. If I can just get into my car and get a shield around it, I can leave the parking lot without being seen or heard.

Cloaking myself in my strongest possible eighth shield, I step out of my door and look down the building to see two of the males standing outside the reception like guards.

They notice my door opening immediately—as well as the lack of any visible person coming out of it.

"There!" one of them shouts.

Shit. They will have been briefed about my abilities. Swearing, I leave the door swinging and make a run for my car.

Footsteps thunder on the pavement behind me as I sprint down the carpark for all I'm worth, my duffel bouncing by my side. I reach the bubble of magic my car is in, open the driver's door and throw myself inside.

The two men hesitate at my lack of appearance, sniffing the air. I turn on the ignition. While they can't see or hear it, they *will* see the way the gravel moves as my tires flee the scene. I've parked rear-in, so I take one deep breath, and put the pedal to the floor.

They shout, pointing directly at me while one of them exclaims into a walkie-talkie. I swear again. *Of course* they've brought back-up. Something heavy lands on my car and in my fright my invisibility shield shatters, and I struggle to gather my wits enough to get it back up.

I head for the road, only to find a black Mercedes screeching to a stop across the driveway, my exit blocked. Another snake gets out of the driver's seat, grinning at his friends.

His expression turns from joyful to horror within seconds, but he's not looking at me. He snarls and bolts past my car.

A high-pitched scream sounds from behind me, and I whirl around in my seat to see a blur of activity. There's another scream followed by a bellowing, then the sound of bodies falling.

I remain in my car, clutching my steering wheel as if it will save me, panting like I've run a marathon. I have no idea what to do now. There's no way for me to drive out.

Everything goes quiet. The hairs on the backs of my arms stand on their ends. I look around, but I can't see anyone.

Until a lion wearing a navy three-piece suit casually strolls around my car, wiping bloody hands on a black pocket handkerchief. His walk is the swagger of a pure apex predator and he comes to a halt directly in front of my car. His amber-eyed stare is menacing and I'm left gaping at him.

I know he's a lion by his tanned, angelic features and the mane to match—long, honey-gold hair tied back into a ponytail at the nape of his neck. He has the look of a put together aristocrat, not a hair askew and definitely out of place in this motel. A bounty hunter maybe? No, not dressed like that, and my father would die before he dealt with lions.

When he speaks, his voice is deep and holds the command of someone used to being obeyed. "Get out of the vehicle, Aurelia." Even with his voice muffled through the glass, my anima demands I submit to his dominance and I struggle with it for a moment.

He knows my name. I hide my fear with a scoff. But he just pins me with his amber eyes and says, "You and I are going to have a chat."

Somehow, he makes me feel like I'm back at school again and I'm in trouble for doing something stupid. He's freezing me with the most lethal glare. He can only be in his late twenties, and fuck, he's hot. Who the hell is he?

Chapter 22

Aurelia

He sighs, as if irritated by me. "I'm not here to hurt you, Aurelia. But if you don't get out of your car, I'm going to tear it to shreds, piece by piece."

Shit.

I have no choice here. I slap my palm to my forehead and swear out loud at my well-laid plans falling apart. Has he heard about the fire? Has it made the news? I haven't yet had the chance to check if it made it into *Animalia Today*. Halfeather was wealthy enough that his death has every right to be on the news.

I look back at the lion, who is glaring at me as if I'm wasting his time. *Shit, Aurelia, we can do this.*

Predator, remember? That's what you are. And we can't let him hurt Maisy.

Slowly, I unlock my car door and push it open. Trying not to tremble, and very aware a six-foot-something ridiculous tall lion is watching my every move, I step out.

The first thing I do is look behind my car, where I find the bloodied bodies of the five serpents. One has a broken neck, but the other four have been disembowelled with long, bloody slashes. I quickly look back at the lion, who has walked two silent steps closer to me since my brief look away from him. I jump a little and take a step back, looking down at his hands where, no doubt, claws had been just a minute ago.

He's killed five of my father's hunting snakes in less than a minute.

I meet his eye and say darkly, "My father will kill you for that."

The corner of his lip quirks, but he does not smile. "Oh, quite a few people try regularly. I rather enjoy sending them back corpses."

Something about his arrogant tone angers me, and I narrow my eyes at him. "Who do you think you are? You can't just come in my motel and—"

"*Your* motel?" He raises an elegant male brow.

I cross my arms and he nods to the buildings behind me. "Incidentally, this is one of *my* motels."

I only just manage to stop my jaw from dropping. "What the fuck?"

"Language, Miss Aquinas," he chides.

I stare at him. He's talking to me like a high school teacher. Who the hell does he think he is?

He must see the crazed look on my face because he says drolly, "My name is Lyle Pardalia. I'm Deputy Headmaster of Animus Academy."

Oh shit. He's come here to retrieve me. They sent the Deputy Headmaster of the prison school *himself*?

"You're not safe here." He looks at my car with a slight curl to the lip, as if he finds it distasteful.

"I know that," I say through gritted teeth, taking great offence. "That's why I was leaving before you interrupted me."

He levels me with a very unimpressed look that has me instantly raging. "You cannot be running around as you are."

Running around?!

"Aurelia." He says my name as if he's reading from a very long, particularly boring shopping list. "Let me help you."

I take a deep breath to calm myself. "How did you find me?"

He leans against Maisy, regarding me like a particularly uninteresting specimen. "Your phone is trackable."

The feeling of pure idiocy that spins through me makes me want to hurl. I can't believe I've been so stupid! Beasts have been hunting each other for hundreds of years and technology has just helped us be more efficient at it.

"Why are you here?"

He looks at his fingernails where blood has crusted around the edges. "Some problematic beasts are after you and you are no longer safe in the wider world."

I frown at him. I know that already. They are a bunch of psychos. But to hear that they *were* actually hunting me is a bleak confirmation that makes my stomach curl into a knot. Did I really think I could out run *them*?

He sighs as if he's explaining something to a stupid person. "You need to come to the Academy where we can keep you safe."

Why does every male around think they own me? I bristle where I stand, meeting him gaze for gaze. I'm not going to *another* place where a man thinks he can control me. "That place is for criminals and feral shifters. I don't belong there."

"I don't care, Aurelia. We need you where we can keep an eye on you while we work to hunt the others. You will be safe there. You can still get your education, we offer a range of healing courses for shifters. That's what you would like to pursue as a career, is it not? Healing?"

He knows a lot more about me than I like. And who's *we*? The Council? Of course they'd have a hand in this now they think I've killed Halfeather. Fuck.

I frown in annoyance at my clenched hands. This male is planning out my life as if I don't have a say in it. But I *do* have some say. On one hand, I'd be safe from my father at the school—students are off bounds to everyone, including court royalty. There'd also be others at the college and means of boosting my power. I also wouldn't have to worry about paying for tuition. Everything at the Academy is Council-funded.

I raise my head and look at this lion—knowing full well they've sent the *Deputy Headmaster* of the Academy for ferals after me because I'm in big bloody trouble. I've never been in trouble for anything before and it's a foreign, gnawing feeling.

But if I go there and they rope up my mates, we'll all be stuck together in one school and I'll be forced to interact with them.

No, there is no way I'm going. I glance at my duffel, still dishevelled in the passenger seat, thinking about how I'm going to make an exit. Lions have a strong instinct to chase, like other predators. If I simply *ran*, he would more than happily chase me down for days. Glancing up at the sky, I see that it's a clear day, practically cloudless. I can do this.

I set my jaw and uncross my arms as if I've given in. "Fine."

"Good." He straightens so smoothly he might have been made from water and turns on his heel, heading to my passenger door to grab my bags, I guess.

"My car is waiting around the corner," he says, pulling a phone out of his pocket. "I'll let the driver know."

I glower at him, darting back into my car through the driver's side and snatching up my bag before he can open the door.

He frowns at me through the windscreen and I shake my head, yanking my bag up and thinking rapidly about what I can carry. Cash. That's all I can manage. The phone is a big loss, but that can't be helped. I shove the wad into my mouth, tearing up as I look around at my beautiful Maisy.

Goodbye for now, old girl.

Lyle is striding down the driveway towards the road, expecting me to follow like an obedient student under his control. Joke's on him because I run in the opposite direction, my wad of cash in my mouth. Lyle lets out a shout as my sneakers pound on the gravel. I take one jump, shifting into my eagle form, my clothes and shoes falling off around me. I frantically beat my wings and Lyle gives a fairly distinct, "Fuck!" That just proves what an asshole he is for telling *me* not to cuss. I ascend into the sky, Lyle's dress shoes rapidly crunching on the gravel after me.

I've guessed right, he's not the type of beast to fully shift in public, not that it matters—I'm in line with the roof of the motel now and I've found a solid beat with my wings. I've also overestimated the size of my beak and the cash slips sideways. I scramble to catch it, trying hard not to lose my wing balance.

It's no use. The cash tumbles out of my beak and I watch it fall straight towards the motel parking lot, where Lyle Pardalia catches it in one broad, tanned hand. He looks back up and there's a truly terrifying expression on his handsome face as he scowls up at me.

Swearing in five different ways, I leave it all behind me and concentrate on beating my wings to get my freedom.

Chapter 23

Aurelia

My eagle form is not a cure-all to my issue. Lyle will have access to the recovery team, which tracks down feral and rabid beasts and takes them to prison, or if they are under twenty-five, to Animus Academy for rehabilitation and education. That recovery team will include winged animalia trained in hunting.

Not knowing how he'd come to find me in the first place, I'm still not safe and I don't know how quickly Lyle is going to get a team together—or how long it'll take him, as a lion, to hunt me down again. It will be embarrassing for him to return without me, and lions have big egos, second only to dragons. He won't stop until he finds me, I just know it.

That just means I have to be cleverer than anyone else.

I focus on gaining as much height as I can and head north, as I'd initially intended. So I don't have my car. This might be a blessing in disguise because travel for me now has no boundaries, and with my eagle sight, I will be able to see anyone coming from land or sky from miles away. If I can find a tall tree to roost in for the night, I can even sleep as a bird for one or two nights. Any more than that and I will likely turn feral myself, letting my anima take over in its animalistic mindset. And all my anima wants to do right now is find my mates. No, my human brain needs to be in control at all times.

I can't believe my awful luck. In the span of a week, I've managed to find three of my mates and the other two know what I look like from my little siren call that one night. And now them, Lyle fucking Pardalia and the Council are hunting me. Savage likely has my scent from that one night of disaster, and if he's following his instincts, he will scent me out in no time on foot.

The image of him standing over me, sucking on his fingers, fills my stomach with tumbling emotions. I want to cry, but I just can't afford to lose focus.

Flying is one of my greatest joys; as an eagle—or

hawk or raven, it's all brilliant. I felt closest to my mother when I was an eagle because, apparently, it was her preferred form. The feeling of the currents shifting below my wings is at once comforting and exhilarating. It feels like true freedom to be up here as an actual bird of prey, capable of simply *seeing* the world in the highest definition. Mice scurried in the fields below me, tiny sparrows flitted through the trees and I even saw to rabbits going at it under a bush. At least *someone* was living their dream and getting some action.

If I'm not careful, it's easy to get lost in the sensation of flying. When I think of this, understanding why animalia become feral or even rabid is not surprising.

But alas, my anima knows that I am not an eagle by nature. I'm getting a little tired because my wing stamina isn't the best as I don't fly very often, so I push myself to get as much distance as possible between myself and what feels like the entire world pursuing me.

Before long, I'm weakening in the dark of night, and though my eagle eyes are brilliant in the dark, I need food and a place to rest while I recover for the next long stretch of travel. I make a slow, controlled descent, following the twinkling lights of a shopping district and heading to the outskirts of that, spotting a small group of half constructed houses.

There has to be a warm, vacant spot there for me to sleep in, undisturbed and hidden. I wheel down, choosing a house that looks like it has only just gotten its bricks set today. Heading in straight to the open entrance, I sigh happily through my beak. I dare not shift back to human form tonight, though. I have no clothes after all, and I imagine a tableau where human builders arrive early in the morning for work and find a naked girl in their construction site.

Huffing, I settle down in a corner, pulling my wings about me to snuggle in for a nap. But even as tiredness pulls me down like a heavy blanket, my heart pounds like I'm still in danger.

Adrenaline spikes through me like a wild wind and I'm on high alert immediately, blinking through the dark. Crickets chirp outside. The wind whistles through the empty house, stirring my feathers just slightly. I smell drying cement and the fresh scent of the wood used the build the frame of this house.

It should be peaceful. But instead, the world around me is buzzing with raw, dangerous energy. Something is nearby. Something powerful.

And then a voice like shadows and dark places

effortlessly pierces my seven shields. *"I've been inside you, princess. You can't hide from us."*

Savage is here.

This is the beginning of *Her Vicious Beasts*, a spicy MFMMMM fated mates contemporary fantasy series.

The story *really* gets going in Book 1, *Her Feral Beasts*.

About the Author

Ektaa P. Bali was born in Fiji and spent most of her life in Melbourne, Australia.

She studied nursing and midwifery at Deakin University, going on to spend eight years as a midwife in various hospitals.

Now, she writes stories about powerful dark goddesses, epic battles in faraway realms and sweeping romances between villains and the clever women they obsess over.

Her Vicious Beasts is her fourth series set in the

Chrysalis-verse and the first in her first New Adult WhyChoose series.

She currently lives in Brisbane, Australia.

facebook.com/ektaabaliauthor
instagram.com/ektaabaliauthor
youtube.com/ektaabali

Also by E.P. Bali

New Adult Fantasy Romance

A Song of Lotus and Lightning Saga:

#1 The Warrior Midwife

#2 The Warrior Priestess

#3 The Warrior Queen

#1 The Archer Princess

#2 The Archer Witch

#3 The Archer Queen

Her Vicious Beasts

#0.5 The Beginning

#1 Her Feral Beasts

#2 Her Rabid Beasts

#3 Her Psycho Beasts

#4 Her Tortured Beasts

#5 Her Monstrous Beasts

Upper YA Dark Fantasy

The Travellers:

#1 *The Chrysalis Key*

#2 *The Allure of Power*

#3 *The Wings of Darkness*

Printed in the USA
CPSIA information can be obtained
at www.ICGtesting.com
LVHW051231111123
763485LV00069B/2475

9 780645 690903